THE SUN'S GOTTEN INTO MY BODY. *It's the core of what I'm writing. A portrait of Eve in the echoes of my room. Sentences that describe her, that draw her out. I'm in love.*

I believe in possibilities. Yes, even here. Even hurtling down our slopes. A word described her for me that day when we raced downward on bikes from the Virgin Mary. That day, right when she told me she would never say I love you, I saw the word that described her, a word at once resonant and foreign in this place: grace. If this grace is part of my possibilities, I thought, I can do anything.

Port Louis looks at me differently. I believed dark, ugly Port Louis, disfigured by grotesque shapes, insurmountable in its waves of human-kind, was beckoning to me. Its black pigeons dotting every roof agreed to decipher its moods for me. The city told me: if there are moments like this one and faces like your own, then, you have to love me, if only for this.

I know this, that I'm only a simulacrum. But a drop of blue ink has gotten into me. I transform it into a black child's ink, lacerating the walls. This story you're reading on my walls, its words will only disappear when the buildings born out of the cyclones' waters have disappeared.

EVE out of
her RUINS

ALSO AVAILABLE IN ENGLISH BY ANANDA DEVI

Indian Tango
translated by Jean Anderson

EVE
OUT OF HER
RUINS

—

Ananda Devi

TRANSLATED FROM THE FRENCH BY
JEFFREY ZUCKERMAN

FOREWORD BY
J.M.G LE CLÉZIO

DEEP VELLUM PUBLISHING
DALLAS, TEXAS

Deep Vellum Publishing

3000 Commerce St., Dallas, Texas 75226

deepvellum.org · @deepvellum

Deep Vellum Publishing is a 501c3
nonprofit literary arts organization founded in 2013.

ISBN: 978-1-941920-40-4 (paperback) · 978-1-941920-41-1 (ebook)
LIBRARY OF CONGRESS CONTROL NUMBER: 2016939553

—

Cover design & typesetting by Anna Zylicz · annazylicz.com

Text set in Bembo, a typeface modeled on typefaces cut by Francesco Griffo
for Aldo Manuzio's printing of *De Aetna* in 1495 in Venice.

Distributed by Consortium Book Sales & Distribution.

Printed in the United States of America on acid-free paper.

Table of Contents

—

The island sometimes fades away like a stain. The island of gilded coastlines, hotels like royal palaces, luxury shops, and dreamlike villas. But it is another island that Ananda Devi describes, an island of dryness and drabness, neighborhoods bereft of hope, areas nobody dares to go: Rochebois, Karo Calyptus, Troumaron. This island never fades away; it is *peyi Moris*, an island of violence and promiscuity, where teenagers have nothing to do but lie in ambush, zip around town on mopeds, pretend to be adults. It's an island where girls are doomed from the start to become "turtles"—women crushed under their husbands' oppression—or to slide into the bottomless ravine carved by prostitution and drugs. Mauritians have coined for those living on this island a name that says everything: *population générale*. Neither this nor that, neither black nor white, neither Creole nor Hindu.

But there is Eve. Eve with a child's body, thin and dark, with a face bearing a small comic-book smile, with a wild mane of hair, thick and tough. Eve who does not accept, who does not submit, who defies her father and the world, who laughs while toying with men's desires. Eve who like a woman knows everything and like a child forgets everything. Eve who gleams because she is the star deep within Troumaron's darkness, a *marrone* escaping from slavery into unfriendly forests and towering buildings. And she is the living, beating heart of this broken world; she is desired by everybody, and she belongs to nobody, except Savita, who took her into her arms one day when she couldn't go home, and who soothed her until she fell asleep, until pure, unchangeable love in all its beauty was born within her.

What can the others, all the others, the teenagers and adults and witnesses and actors, do? The island is their prison, the beautiful coastlines tug at their heart, even as they dream of escaping some-day, going far away, to the other shore, going where people drive beautiful new cars and live all alone in houses with ten rooms, far from the ugly slums and rusted buses, away from the streets where heat sticks to bodies and ennui flows through veins like cruelty. The bars of their prison are made of envy and hate. Someday they will get up, and they will demand answers. Or take empty bottles and rags soaked in gas and make Molotov cocktails to throw—at who? for what? Clélio will stay in jail, despite his lawyer, despite his witnesses who took wing over his building's roof, even as deep within a cellar Savita...And so everyone will stay put, the beautiful coastlines will keep on shimmering like a frilly dress around royal palaces, the IRS—the Integrated Revenue System—will go on helping those *gran mounes*, pretentious people with pretentious lives, and men will go on stalking barely pubescent girls' bodies and pushing them down to the ground, down to their knees.

Yet Eve has truth on her side, and so she overcomes everything, truth is her ally even in her final revenge. For her, those who have eyes can see the truth, a thing worth far more than all the images and all the legends of the world. Before doing what cannot be undone, the murder that puts an end to the adults' abuses and her father's punches, she cuts off her mane to look like a lioness. For her, Savita will do anything, even die, and Saad will bear the responsibility for her crime, because he loves her as if nobody's serious at seventeen. Ananda Devi—who knows the cost of waging war against institutional wrongs and capricious fate as she delineates this battle in every one of her books—makes her island a fiery star on the maps of the Indian Ocean.

She forces open a door in darkness's wall. This opening indeed reveals the beauty of the island, of this gift from the gods that is Mauritius, this gift that humans do not deserve but only a few innocents may ever see. "To the west," says Saad, "there's the harbor, so calm in the morning that we can't see the least ripple in the water. That's the first miracle: water that could almost be walked on." Come and join them, take off your useless finery, forget all your prejudices; only then will you experience these other miracles and one day, like Saad, pull Eve out of her ruins.

Jean-Marie Gustave Le Clézio
translated by Jeffrey Zuckerman

EVE

Walking is hard. I limp, I hobble along on the steaming asphalt. With each step a monster rises, fully formed.

The urban night swells, elastic, around me. The salty air from the Caudan waterfront scrapes my wounds and my skin, but I go on.

I clear my own path. What was once deep within me—the slow drip of life that has slipped away and turned me into this livid creature sucking the night dry—no longer matters. The silence that fills me takes my breath away.

I'm getting into my stride. I no longer have a choice. I can only hear the stuttering beat of my footsteps. I hoist my schoolbag on my right shoulder; there aren't just books in it tonight. There's a reassuring bulge right next to my armpit: the blaze of false starts and missed arrivals. Soon enough it will no longer be a rhythm coursing through my veins. I'm going to leave my mark on a forehead, right between the eyebrows. I was born for this moment.

I wipe my neck. The coarse feel of it surprises me. The lack of hair makes me feel more naked than ever. Then I remember: my mother sheared it off. When I saw myself in the mirror, I saw that I had a lioness's head. I had a mane of hunger.

I walk, even if I'd rather run toward myself. The night quivers. The city trembles. I have gone. Nothing can stop me now.

PART ONE

SAAD

I am Saadiq. Everybody calls me Saad.

Between despair and cruelty the line is thin.

Eve is my fate, but she claims not to know it. When she bumps into me, her gaze passes through me without stopping. I disappear.

I'm in a gray place. Or rather, yellowish brown, which better suits its name: Troumaron. Troumaron, a sort of funnel; where all the island's wastewaters ultimately flow. Here is where the cyclone refugees are rehomed, those rendered homeless by tropical storms and who, two or five or ten or twenty years later, still have their toes in the water and their eyes pale as rain.

I've always lived there. I was born a refugee. Like everyone else who's grown up in the yellow shadows of these buildings, I've never understood their monstrous edges. I never saw the gaps born beneath our feet, separating us from the world. I played with Eve. We called her the skeleton because she was so thin, but also to mask an unspoken affection. We played at war until we found ourselves at war.

We are at the bottom of Signal Mountain. Port Louis grabs our feet but we are stuck here. The city turns its back on us. Its muted magma stops at our borders. The mountain blocks our view of other things. Between the city and the stone are our buildings, our rubble, our trash. The eczema of paint and the tar beneath our feet. A children's playground has become a battleground teeming with needles, shards of broken glass, hopes snaking into nothing. Here, boys clenched their fists for the first time, and girls cried for the first time. Here, everyone has faced up to their realities.

One day we wake up and the future has disappeared. The sky hides the windows. Night makes its way into our bodies and refuses to leave.

Night and our hormones gone wild. We boys are bundles of frustration. We start following girls to the shuttered factory that devoured our mothers' dreams. Maybe that's also what's waiting for them. There's nothing left of the factory but an empty metal shell and hundreds of sewing machines that carved into their shoulders that curve of despair and into their hands those nicks and cuts like tattoos. The remnants of every woman who worked here linger. We see that they tried to bestow some humanity on this desolation. Beside each machine, there's a mauve plastic flower, yellowing family photos, postcards from Europe, and even a forgotten red barrette, a strand of hair still caught in it. And religious symbols—crucifixes, Koranic verses, Buddha statues, Krishna figures—that would allow us to guess which community they belonged to, if we wanted to play such guessing games. When the factory closed down, they weren't even allowed to retrieve their things. It was that abrupt, that unexpected, but I realized, later, that they hadn't wanted to see any of it. I wonder what use all this piety was to them. In any case, all of it was left to rust and to our perverse games behind the moldy curtains. These are our traces, in these stale, dingy rooms. Stains of so many virginities lost here.

Sometimes, when the neighborhood is quiet, the island's sounds seem different. Other kinds of music, less funereal tones, the clang of cash registers, the dazzle of development. The tourists scorn us without realizing it. Money has made them naïve. We cheat them out of a few rupees until they begin to mistrust our pleasant, false faces.

The country puts on its sky-blue dress, the better to seduce them. A marine perfume wafts from its crotch. From here we can't see the island all dolled up, and their eyes, dazzled by the sun, can't see us. As things should be.

Mothers disappear in a resigned haze. Fathers find in alcohol the virtue of authority. But they don't have that anymore, authority. Authority, that's us, the boys. We've recruited our troops like military leaders. We've carved out our portions of the neighborhood. Once our parents stopped working, we became the masters. Everybody knows we can't be ordered around. And now nobody can look us in the eyes without shivering. From that moment, each of us began to live as he wanted to, free from everything, free from rules. We make the rules.

But something else has slipped into my dreams lately. I mark the walls of my room with my questions; I bloody them with the juice of words. I learn to be quiet. I learn to talk to myself. I learn to put myself together and to take myself apart. I suppose we're all like that; we go with the flow, like the others, but inside, each of us withdraws into himself and harbors his secrets. I follow in their steps and I act like I belong, as a matter of form, as a matter of survival. Eve doesn't understand that.

Eve walks by, her hair like foamy night, in her skin-tight jeans, and the others snigger and suck their teeth in lust, but I—I want to kneel down. She doesn't look at us. She isn't afraid of us. She has her solitude for armor.

At night, my hormones seize on her face and describe it in long arcs of desire. When I can't bear it anymore, I go out with the gang, our noisy mopeds tormenting the sleepy old folk. In the morning, the others sink into the stupor of drugs and rage. But I go take a shower, I shave, and I go to class. This double life sucks me dry, yet nothing in the world could keep me from seeing Eve's profile in the morning at the bus stop, a sliver of sunlight playing on her ear.

And then, I swear, I love words.

I slip a poetry book into her bag.

Later, she bumps into me and her eyes bore through me. It drives me insane.

To her I dedicate all the sentences that have been darkening my walls. To her I dedicate all my bitter suns.

Our *cité* is our kingdom. Our city in the city, our town in the town. Port Louis has changed shape; it has grown long teeth and buildings taller than its mountains. But our neighborhood hasn't changed. It's the last bastion. Here, we let our identities happen: we are those who do not belong. We call ourselves *bann Troumaron*—the Troumaronis—as if we were yet another kind of people on this island filled with so many kinds already. Maybe we actually are.

Our lair, our playground, our battleground, our cemetery. Everything is there. We don't need anything else. One day we'll be invincible and the world will tremble. That's our ambition.

EVE

Pencil. Eraser. Ruler. Paper. Gum. I played blind man's bluff with the things I wanted. I was a child, but not entirely. I was twelve years old. I shut my eyes and held out my hand. My fingers closed on air. I shivered in my thin clothes. I thought everything was within reach. I made moonlight shine in the boys' eyes. I believed I had powers.

Pencil. Eraser. Ruler. I held out my hand because in my bag there was nothing. I went to school completely and totally empty. I felt some kind of pride in not having anything. People can be rich even in having nothing.

Because I was small, because I was thin, because my arms and my legs were as straight as a child's drawing, the bigger boys protected me. They gave me what I wanted. They thought a gust of wind would tip me over like a paper boat with a leak in its side.

I was a paper boat. Water seeped into my sides, my stomach, my legs, my arms. I didn't know it. I thought I was strong. I weighed up my chances. Assessed every moment. I knew how to ask without seeming to.

Pencil, eraser, ruler, it didn't matter. The boys gave me things. Their faces softened slightly, and that changed everything, it made them look human. And then, one day, when I asked without seeming to, they asked me for something in return.

I thought it would be simple, it would be easy. What could they want in return? I was the smallest one, the least important one. Everyone knew I had nothing. For once, they were saying I had something. My bag held many nothings: the nothingness of my apartment, smaller and more bare than everyone else's; the empty nothingnesses of our wardrobes; even those of our trash cans. There was the nothing of my father's eye, which alcohol had turned oily. The nothing that was my mother's mouth and eyelids, both of them stapled shut. I had nothing, nothing at all to give.

But I was mistaken.

He wanted a piece of me.

He dragged me off to a corner of the playground, behind a huge Indian almond tree, he pinned me against the tree's trunk, and he slipped his hand under my T-shirt. I was wearing a red T-shirt, with a soccer player's name on it. I don't remember who anymore. His hand stopped at my breasts, slowly moved up and down, just over the small black points. There was hardly anything there. I heard other children shouting and playing. They seemed far away. It was another world. The boy had slipped his other hand in. His skin turned blotchy. His cheek was hot. He took his time, even though he was scared. But I didn't feel anything. I was out of my body. It was apart from me.

That day, he didn't ask me for anything else. He gave me an eraser, or a pencil, or a notebook, I don't remember. His lips came close to my ear. The next time, he said, we'll try something else.

I shrugged, but I stared with some curiosity at his eyes. They had a silver sheen like melted sugar. As if he had been erased. Now he only existed through his hands. Now he only existed through me.

For the first time my bag was no longer empty. I had something I could pay with: myself.

I could buy. Exchange myself for what I needed. Exchange morsels, bits, various parts of my body. I looked brazenly at the taller boys when school was let out. You want to see something? I asked them. They laughed and said, Go away, there's nothing to see. But then they looked at me a long while and my eyes told them something else. I knew how to do it. Someone else slipped fluidly into my gaze, someone completely separate from my bony body. I refused to be small or weak. I contradicted myself. That changed everything. They stopped breathing. They flowed into the shadows on my face. They left caresses there, a slime of desire that oozed down my right cheek. They, the bigger boys, had something else to give in return: books, calculators, CDs. All I gave them was the shadow of a body.

I am in permanent negotiation. My body is a stop-over. Entire sections have been explored. Over time, they blossom with burns and cracks. Everyone leaves some trace, marks his territory.

I am seventeen years old and I don't give a fuck. I'm buying my future.

I am transparent. The boys look at me like they can see me inside out. The girls avoid me like a sickness. My reputation's been sealed.

I'm alone. But I've known for a long while the value of solitude. I walk straight ahead, untouchable. Nobody can read anything on my blank face, except what I choose to show. I'm not like the others. I don't belong to Troumaron. The neighborhood didn't steal my soul like the other drones that live there. This skeleton has a secret life sealed in its belly. It's carved by the sharp edge of refusal. Neither the past nor the future matter; they don't exist. And the present doesn't either.

EVE OUT OF HER RUINS

Eraser. Pencil. Ruler. Beginnings are always easy. And then we open our eyes to a bleak world, to a universe under siege. The looks of others, eyes that judge and condemn. I'm seventeen and I've decided my life.

I'm braving the reefs all around me. I won't be like my mother. I won't be like my father. I'm something else, something not really alive. I walk alone, straight ahead. I'm not afraid of anybody. They're the ones who fear me, who fear what they can only guess lies beneath my skin.

The more they touch me, the more they lose hold of me. The ones who dare to look into my eyes feel dizzy. They're so simple. The inexplicable frightens them. They have fixed ideas. A girl to marry, a girl to conquer and toss aside. Those are the only two categories they can understand. But I don't belong to one or the other. So they end up baffled and angry.

At night, I haunt the asphalt. Meetings are arranged. They take me, they bring me back. I remain cold. Whatever changes in me, it's not the truest, innermost part of myself. I protect myself. I know how to protect myself from men. I'm the predator here.

They take me. They bring me back. Sometimes, they rough me up. No matter. It's just a body. It can be fixed. That's what it's for.

I sidestep the traps and the obstacles. I dance in evasion.

Shadow or wing, what you were no longer is. You become something else. In Troumaron, a reflection follows you. It taunts you. It tells you you're walking the wrong way. It transforms your surfaces, inverts your trajectory, reveals the other side of your silence. The paper boat is leaking everywhere and you don't know it. You watch as you sink but you don't see that it's you. Erasers, papers, pencils, rulers, books, heart, kidneys, toes. One day, you'll see yourself in the mirror, and nothing at all will be yours.

You see a face congealed under its lies. You ask yourself where you went. You were looking for a key—but something had broken in.

CLÉLIO

I'm Clélio. I'm at war. Fighting everybody and nobody. I can't get away from my rage. Someday, I know it, I'll kill someone. Dunno who. Maybe my parents, or some boss, or one of my guys, or a girl, or myself. Dunno who. I'm Clélio. You know who I am, so don't you mess with me. You shitheads have no idea what anger is if you've never met me.

I've done all sorts of jobs. The only one left is to kill someone. And then sometimes I sing. When I sing, people listen. Well, at least they stop. I stop their lives and their hearts. My voice pierces infinity, Saad told me. (He doesn't talk like anyone else here.) My voice makes metal shiver, apparently. The buildings stop crushing men, cement loosens its grip. Walls turn nostalgic. Girls go rosy. But I won't fucking sing for shit.

A couple of times they've asked me to sing at a wedding. Everyone just stares at me, beaming like idiots, and I want to punch their faces in. To see them standing around in their nice clothes. Their shoes so tight their toes look ready to pop out like horns. And they're acting like nothing's wrong, stuffing their mouths and boozing like they're not miserable and broke—it makes me want to shove those smiles down their throats. I tell myself that if one more old lady asks me to sing *Marinella*, I'm kicking her straight to hell. I'm no good when I drink too much. One beer and I'll knock over the tables and the bride. One time I even jumped on the bride to pull off her veil, because I knew it was a mask. If they hadn't held me back, I'd have pulled away her dress, too, and all the oaths she'd taken.

I must have been born that way. I must have seen the future and decided I didn't like it. So when I see nails, I feel like swallowing them or forcing someone else to swallow them.

I've been through prison for assault and battery many times. I wasn't ever there for long, since I'm a minor. Next year, when I'm eighteen, the punishments will be worse. The judges, if they're men, lecture me. If they're women, they go weak when they see how my eyes look like a kid's; they go soft and try to tell me, implore me to do better. I know I won't change, though. I'm a little snot. A little shit.

I am Clélio. Dirt poor bastard, swallower of everyone else's rusty nails. What can you do? Nobody changes just like that.

SAAD

They tell me I'll succeed. But success does not mean the same thing for everyone. It's a slippery word. In my case, it simply means that locked doors could open just a bit and I could, if I sucked in my stomach, slip through and escape Troumaron. Everybody knows poverty is the harshest of jailers. Still, the teachers say everything is possible. They tell me how they, too, once learned their lessons by candlelight. But I can see in their eyes just how dim their minds are as a result. They insist: seize your opportunities, don't hold back your country. But who do they mean by "your"?

Stereotypes were made for us. We fill them all. We are the champions.

The teachers allude to success, as if they were talking to me without entirely believing what they were saying. They look at me surreptitiously: You can make miracles happen. It's true, I have a good memory. I'm a sponge: I absorb everything. And I'm a bladder: I pour everything back out. Apparently that helps for success. Swallow and expel.

But I make good use of them. I go to class. I pass my tests. I lead a double life: night with the gang, day with the sages.

I can still remember the day I split into two. During French class, the teacher, a young woman with skin as jaundiced as her canary-yellow blouses and who didn't stay for long (and for that reason I say she was only there for me, at that moment, like fate knocking on my sleepy head), the teacher said: We're going to read poems by someone your age. As soon as they heard the word poetry, the boys pretended to retch and covered up their ears while making rude noises. But she read those poems anyway, in the middle of this ruckus, and also this boy's letters, in her small, trembling voice. She started: *No one's serious at seventeen*. At first, I thought to myself, he's wrong; for us, seventeen is very serious. But then I heard, instead of her feminine voice, the harsh voice of a teenager talking about his hopes, his rebellion, his wounds, his wishes, and even more than that, he was talking about the world, his and mine, and suddenly I felt keenly that he was talking to me and only me. Yes, directly to me. He was saying, I am your brother. She read a poem where he was saying that vowels had colors, and the truth of it made me sit bolt upright: I, too, saw colors in words. Just as the island unfurled its blues and oranges, so the words unfurled still more vividly purple rages in my head. When she was done she said, this poet's name is Rimbaud.

I am your brother.

I am your double. I am your single. I have split completely and totally in two: I was Saad, sitting transfixed in my stiff chair (or stiff in my transfixed chair), and I was someone else, unmoored, observing things but pushing them away through his thoughts, his defiance, his mortality.

That night, lying in bed, I took a marker and began writing on the wall by my head. Of course, I wrote about Eve. She alone occupied my thoughts. I began talking to her directly, saying *you* instead of *she*, guessing where she's going, what she's thinking, what she's living. She doesn't know that I've figured her out. I've written so much about her that sometimes I think I'm actually writing her life, and other people's lives, and all our lives.

I read in secret, all the time. I read in the toilets, I read in the middle of the night, I read as if books could loosen the noose tightening around my throat. I read to understand that there is somewhere else. A dimension where possibilities shimmer.

EVE

The water and its swirls. Its lines, its marbling, its abrupt changes in direction. I spend hours watching the stream run endlessly. Colors slip beneath its clarity when the sun hits it straight on. And I do too, I slip forward, carried by time, by nothing.

The buildings are straight ahead. I'm not afraid of them. I dare them to look back at me. All of us born there are fated to die, but that doesn't mean anything. Everybody is born to that fate. The babies' eyes are drained of color and sky. I've known for a long time the coldness of metal. It's imbued me with its liquid strength.

This neighborhood was a marsh at the base of the mountain. They filled it in to build these streets, but they couldn't do anything about the smell of wrack or the unsteadiness of the ground where only the corpses of brambles and dreams are still growing. Several buildings are starting to tilt. Soon, we'll have our own Leaning Tower of Pisa. The eighth wonder of the world: Troumaron.

Seated on a mound not far off, I'm smoking and watching them. There's a guard at the end of each street. The fiery tips of their joints dot the closed circle. The boys swear oaths, declare rules, make alliances: a pack mentality. If you care about your life, your body, if you're a girl, if you're old, you'd do best to give them a wide berth. They spread a pool of oil around them in which their bored faces and their footsteps are reflected. Now, nobody walks. Everybody runs. It's a dance to the death. According to them, most females carry the same heaviness: this hole that is an impassable yet open door that keeps its secrets. So they go and hunt, like the hundreds of feral dogs raging through the city and tearing it apart.

Even Saad, who's a little different, who thinks about something other than spreading our thighs, is part of a gang. He's afraid to stand out, to be alone, to go off in another direction. He has no idea what's in us.

This troubled water, this murky world, this faraway smile like a moonlit night, when the wind comes to whisper things that make us pensive and sad.

Saad talks about poetry when we're alone. But he has no idea about the poetry of women.

The poetry of women is when Savita and I walk together step by step to avoid the ruts. It's when we pretend to be twins because we look like each other. We wear the same clothes, the same perfume, as if we're dancing together. Our earrings chime. Her nose is pierced with a tiny jewel like a star. The poetry of women is laughter in this lost place, laughter that opens up a small part of paradise so we don't drown ourselves.

But those moments are brief. When I am alone, I sink back into my darkness and I know I will die.

I decide to go back. The stream isn't deep, but I'd rather stay there and listen to its voice than the jeers I'll hear as I walk past.

I see Saad among them. He pretends not to see me. I know he's ashamed. I smile.

A hand has closed around your ankle and is slowly pulling you down. Your eyes skitter. At first, you thought that these gestures and actions were circumscribed. You thought that they were delimited by the rush of desire. But violence came into the equation. And the hand is pulling you, and desire is turning into something else. The act takes on other forms, other furies. There's always more. Possibilities proliferate.

No more hasty couplings behind trees or in bathrooms. You're caught in secret places you never knew about beneath the veneer of ordinary life. A hand drags you along. In the darkness, you don't recognize mouths or shapes. In the darkness, the pain is unexpected. Or in the red light of a bare room you see who has been waiting for you, and your heart falters.

When you go back out you walk in the city slowly, as if you've been knocked off-center. You walk to rid yourself of memories. You open your mouth and let in a hot wind that burns away the danger of remembering. You go back in to sleep, believing you've forgotten it all. You can do it again, without knowing why.

The hand around your ankle doesn't let you go. Its grip tightens. You have no choice now. You can only scrub your burdened flesh again and again, without realizing that you're also erasing your own self.

Forgetfulness is the common link between day and night, the smooth wall that protects you from yourself. You go deaf. You no longer hear the roaring that once tormented your ears. You no longer hear the music in total contradiction to what you see.

SAAD

Baby won't you give it to me, give it to me, you know I want it.

They shake their hips to the song, hardly a movement, a wave that pulls them together, pulls them away, pulls them together again. As they sway, their jeans hug their butts like two hands glued to their curves.

Baby won't you give it to me...

They both wear tank tops, one of them red, the other white, over their small, juicy breasts.

I sit deep in an armchair as their movements blur with the music and the beer, all coursing through me, a liquid pulse surging in my torso. The bass tones reverberate in my groin. If I move at all I'll get hard.

Eve and Savita are dancing together. They aren't looking at us. They aren't looking at anyone. An arabesque of cigarette smoke escapes their lips. Their shoulders shake in rhythm. Their jeans tighten in the same rhythm. I imagine them slipping into the fold, into the crease.

I can't take it anymore. I get up and run down the stairs to the bathrooms. I step over bodies. At the top of this nightclub in Grand Baie there are rooms. I can't stop thinking about Eve and me going up there. We'd open the window because the room would reek of old bodies. Grand Baie's salty air would flow in, turn the brothel room into a small honeymoon suite, everything in red. I'd slip my hand into her jeans. I'd slip music into her legs, onto her shoulders. I'd slip a cigarette between her lips. I'd be the wind, everywhere within her. I'd leave a sheen of salt on her skin.

The music changes, becomes more pressing, but in my head it stays *won't you give it to me, give it to me, you know I want it*, I hum *I want it I want it I want it*, and my hands are furious.

My face is covered in sweat. I walk out of the bathroom, and I'm the one who's reeking. But I feel better. I go back to the nightclub where they're still dancing, unaware that a volcano has just erupted.

I pick up my beer again. The others make fun of me. They talk about her, mock her, sing dirty songs. Eve takes her pants off faster than her own shadow, they say. I don't listen to them. I'm the only one who knows what Eve really is.

Nobody knows what pulls Eve and Savita to each other. Eve and Savita are the two sides of the moon. Savita also lives in Troumaron, but there's a gulf between the two families. Savita's family acts like they don't belong in Troumaron, as if they were only there by accident. The accident of poverty, of course. It's always the same story: the father betting on horses, the mother scrubbing hospital floors. He inhales the stallions' sweat, she smells rotting bodies and blood. Savita doesn't seem to worry about any of that. When they run into each other on the street, Savita's family looks away from Eve as if they'd just seen two dogs in heat, but still the two girls' eyes meet and lock on one another. There's a smile so vague and discreet that you'd have to be looking for it. This smile between the two of them, bronze eyes meeting black, a quiver of light that disappears before it starts to gleam, almost a shared rivulet linking their lips, this smile is a doorway toward a place only the two of them know. Just between girls: we sparring cocks wouldn't know anything about it.

At night in Grand Baie, the world flips inside out like a glove.

The small beachside town swarming with tourists and bonhomie during the day teems with these insects who only come out at night. With scantily clad girls and men turned into wolves, the hunt can begin. The nightclubs turn into labyrinths where deals are made in all languages—English, French, Italian, German, Russian. The identical girls get younger and younger. The smallest ones are from Madagascar or Rodrigues; they can't be more than thirteen. They wait patiently, some without moving at all, others trying to entice the first tourists who come in. I'm ashamed and angry.

They don't have any choice.

But her? Don't tell me there isn't a way out for her. Don't tell me there aren't any possibilities. She's roaming around, looking for the seediest parts, the trenches. I've tried to imagine the horizon as she sees it. I'm sure that's what's driving her, an illusion of light, a country only she can see. I know she's not a station where every bus stops. If everyone else talks about her that way, it's to pull free of her spell, because they're all obsessed with her but no one can have her.

I go back home and sulk over her for days on end. She acts like she doesn't notice anything at all.

Baby won't you give it to me...

No, after all that, I'd rather go back to Rimbaud: *The girls always go to church, glad / To hear the boys call them sluts.*

Slut, slut, slut.

It's a beautiful word in French: *garce.*

Later, I copy out another line for her on the wall in front of her apartment: *This is the rag of disgust that has been shoved in my mouth.* I don't know if I'm talking about her or me. Or even Troumaron.

CLÉLIO

After the soccer game, a bigger guy shoves me. I grab him by his shit-yellow collar and push right back. If he falls, it'd be a fight in the stadium. And it'd be old enemies facing off, as if our teams were still called the Muslim Scouts or the Hindu Cadets. But my friends run over to hold me back and pull my hands off this stinking heap of flesh. I stare at him like I'll rip his face off. They're dragging me away before I set off a fight. But I'd love to. The feeling of hitting someone, taking a blow, enjoying my fury in full force like an acrid wind rushing through me and wiping away my memories.

They won't let me. They drag me toward the city, toward our prison. I get on Kenny's moped. Before he can stop me, I'm gone. I take a long winding route through Port Louis, lit up by its hot dust, I go along the Rue la Corderie where the smell of salted fish fills my nostrils, take a shortcut up the Rue Wellington, go down the Rue la Poudrière where I wave to the old ghosts of whores behind the stone walls, and I come back along the Champ de Mars, where the Citadel watches me with its black eye. On the way, I bang into people, ride on sidewalks, weave past cars, manage not to get knocked over by buses belching black smoke. All the insults blur together. I laugh, people notice, everyone's staring at me. I flip them off, I scrape an SUV, its bumpers big enough to push off nonexistent buffalo, with a little lady behind a steering wheel bigger than she is. She sees me dragging a key across the brand-new car, rolls down her window, but once I get to her and smile, she doesn't say a word, I lick my lips and she blushes, yes,

I'm telling you, she blushes and rolls the window back up to shut out the cool air that had been blowing across my face. Her face crumples up like she's about to cry, it's not pretty at all, the lady in her arctic monster with a heart so soft she can't even yell at me. I blow her a kiss with my fingertips and memorize her license plate and go my way with a smile.

Things are swirling around in my head. Port Louis is sucking something out of me. Too many people, too many cars, too many buildings, too much smoked glass, too many nouveaux-riches, too much dust, too much heat, too many wild dogs, too many rats. I don't know where to go. I keep going round and round. Like I'll bite off my tail.

My older brother Carlo is gone. He went to France ten years ago. I was little. He was my hero. When he left, he said: I'll come back to find you. I'm waiting for him. He never came back. He calls sometimes, but only to make small talk. I don't know what he's doing over there. But when I hear his voice, I know he's lying, that he hasn't done well. When I hear his voice, I know he's dead.

And I'd love to kill, too.

EVE

The rag of disgust. Yes, it was shoved into my mouth when I was born, too.

Standing by the window, I spit cigarette smoke into the night. I watch it dissolving as if it was carrying part of myself away. My mother, when she comes into my room after agonizing in front of the closed door, won't say anything, won't feel anything. She's deliberately insulated herself so as not to feel or regret life. She'd like to be protected from all the mess. But maybe that's all anyone born in the pits of poverty can ever hope for.

Her attempts to cover up the apartment's ugliness with cutouts from old calendars or magazines are pitiful. All over the cement walls are pictures of Mount Fuji with a charming Japanese woman in the foreground, Swiss hills with cows cleaner than most people I know, an etching of Napoleon crowning himself, a photo of young Queen Elizabeth holding a sweet pinkish baby in her arms, and several of Johnny Hallyday all sweaty in leather, leaning crookedly into his microphone. The plastic chairs are red, blue, yellow, and green, the colors of the Mauritian flag, and in the corner is a faux leather couch from her mother. On a Formica table is the one thing that makes her happy: a TV with VCR that fills her days with its yapping. In the kitchen there's practically nothing but cans of corned beef and Glenryck pilchards, some stale bread and macaroni and sardines. She doesn't cook for the family. Everybody feeds themselves. I barely ever eat anything myself. I toast a piece of bread right over the stove flame until it's nearly burned and I eat it after dipping it in some tea. Or maybe it's a few sugar cookies with a little butter spread on. I don't really care.

She's always wrapped in fabrics with ugly prints on them. She forgets she's a woman. What she actually is, I don't know.

I don't want her faux leather, her Brazilian soap operas, her feeble dreams. I've always told my parents no. It was actually the first word I said. You don't know how to say yes? my father asked when I was old enough to understand. No, I said. The slap came before I saw it. It was the first one. I must have been four. After that the slaps, like the windows facing walls, like the pictures tacked up, became part of my everyday life.

But I'm walking backwards, away from that life. As it recedes, my father's face, red in anger, looks silly. The burn disappears quickly, but the memory of it doesn't.

A rag of disgust. It doesn't end there. Every night, sentences keep hammering the landing.

What color is your laugh? I've never seen it. You have two holes to bleed from. You're my little Tom Thumb on your bloody path. I'll follow you to find the traces of our faces.

I'm pissing gold over the towers. They're drowning in twilight and ammonia.

Come with me and I'll be the death of you.

Of course I know it's Saadiq sounding these echoes in the building and setting me a new riddle every night that I refuse to answer.

I don't want to play this game. At night I read the poetry book and I see where his inspiration came from. I don't need his secondhand words.

When I read the book he gave me, the words dance and try to ensnare me. But then I lock up all those thoughts and the book falls out of my hands because of the stone in my heart.

I sleep. I wake up. Mold seeps into my room. The shower next door drips all night. Humidity seeps through the walls. I feel like I'm the one seeping through. I hear my father shoving my mother around. I hear my mother's apathy. Tomorrow her arms will be black and blue. Tomorrow, she'll walk with a waddle. Tomorrow, he'll have sulfurous eyes and he'll smell harsh, like a man.

I'm pissing gold over the towers, I'm humming in the morning loud enough for him to hear. He looks at me sharply.

One night, he came into my room. I pretended to sleep. He watched me. He stayed a long while.

I don't know what he was thinking about, what was going through his head. Is he still a father? Am I still his child? What would I know?

Since then, I've been leaving my underwear lying around to keep him out. I know that makes him upset and worried. He doesn't know what to make of it.

But this frustration keeps swelling, like a tide. My calmness won't last.

SAAD

The day I say I love you to a man, I'll kill myself, she says with a rising laugh.

The road is also rising. Early one morning, I drag her to bikes I borrowed without asking. I take her to the Virgin Mary monument on the mountainside. Up there, the sky is almost blushing shyly under our gaze. This sky that had seen everything was being demure. That's what I was able to show her: something different from our neighborhood. A view of something other than the dryness of gray nights.

To the west there's the harbor, so calm in the morning that we can't see the least ripple in the water. That's the first miracle: water that could almost be walked on. That's the beginning of our fantasy, the threshold of our dreams. The boats no longer carrying passengers seem to be calling us anyway, telling us to come and glide over the water. Or they spread wings instead of sails and soar into the sky. And the two of us, astonished children, up high. The city's chaotic outlines muted, all greens and blues and oranges, is the second miracle. It looks like the city our grandfathers talk about when men took in the sunrise barefoot on their doorsteps, and listened to smiling passersby and hungry martins in the mango trees. We drank up this sunlight like syrup, they said, before it became burning hot. It started your morning off right, just like a bit of rum in your belly. Of course, that didn't keep us from actually drinking a little rum too, two suns in the body are better than one, wouldn't you say?

Here is your city, I say to her quietly. Right here in my hand.

Have a taste of its salty juice. Look into the eyes of the Citadel. It streaks the sky with its refusal.

Then we mount our stolen, no, borrowed bikes, and we race each other down the steep slopes. She doesn't hold back, of course. She looks at me with a smirk as wide as a frog's and turns her back on me and lets herself go at full speed. I follow her. The wind, already warm, whistles against our cheeks. Her hair is already flying back. She shrieks and laughs all at once. At the bottom, we pedal with all our strength to go back up the lane and down the next one. We're slick, immediately, completely, with sweat.

Suddenly, as she's going at full speed, one of her wheels hits a rut and she loses control. I speed up to try to catch her, already seeing her crashing into the ground, a small pile of metal and flesh, but she falls left onto a patch of grass at the very bottom of the slope. I come to a stop near her, terrified, but she's laughing.

I get off my bike and throw myself on her, pinning her to the grass. I feel her body shaking, whether in laughter or fear I don't know. Her sweat smells good. She isn't wearing much clothing and I can feel all her bones and all the hollows in her flesh. The effect is immediate. I bury my nose in the space between her neck and her shoulder.

Tell me you love me, I say.

She answers: The day I say I love you to a man, I'll kill myself.

She's the one with her arms spread out as on a cross, but I'm the one crucified by her words.

I don't know if she realizes it, but she pulls herself free and gets back on the bike.

Thanks for the trip, she says as she leaves.

The waist of her jeans is slung low, revealing a strip of golden-brown flesh and the black outline of a g-string. Her hair hides her back. I'd have liked to lap her up.

On the way back, the gang grills me. What did I do, what happened, what did she say? They see through my lies and laugh at me. Everybody's done her but you, they say, with some sympathy. But they know that doesn't make a difference, and in the end they leave me alone. With my love, my infanta, my queen.

Nobody knows that it's possible to love like that at seventeen. I swim in the night waters of Eve. I plunge into her murky gaze. I drown in her sludge, in her innocence. I don't care who she is, what she does. I'm the winking navel over her jeans' low waist. I'm the curved heel of her bare foot in her sandals. I'm the memory of her all-too-rare laugh, of her strength, of her willfulness.

I don't see anyone else. The sentences on my walls are no longer written in black but in white, and the pen fills and empties all by itself, in incredible spurts.

EVE

The teacher looks at me with a gritted smile. He's nice to me, but shifty. I know he pays attention to the slightest changes in my eyes, my voice, my silence. Open the smallest gap, and he'll plunge right in. I see him coming and I wait. I need tutoring for my tests. He'll do it.

No need to judge me. I follow my own laws. If you came from Troumaron you'd know that. The only thing that keeps me alive is Savita. When we go out together we whisper so intimately that we can smell the alcohol on each other's breath. Phoenix beer has such a sweet taste this way. A hint of foam outlines the upper edge of her purple lips. Our hands, when they touch, fit together perfectly. We move in the same way, with the same rhythm. No need for us to look to know what the other is thinking.

It started the day Savita found me under a tree in the schoolyard. I hadn't been in class. I must have caught some kind of infection. I was shaking, my teeth were chattering, I was cold. I think I had pissed myself. It happened so quickly that I hadn't been able to do anything. My whole body had rebelled and refused to function. She took off her jacket and put it on my shoulders. She didn't say anything to me, like What's wrong with you? or What did you do? or You were asking for it, she said nothing. She helped me to stand up and we walked back together. She smelled like spice and smog. I know my face was gaunt and my cheeks were blotchy, like children when they've done something wrong.

I told her: I don't want to go back home.

She told me that she couldn't take me home because of her

parents, but she would stay with me until I was ready to leave. We sat by the stream. She didn't seem to notice the sharp odor I had. I don't know when exactly I put my head on her knees and fell asleep. She didn't move at all. When I opened my eyes, I saw her clear eyes above mine.

What is it? I asked.

I'm thinking about what you're going through, she said.

You're wrong, I said, I'm not going through anything. I chose my life.

She answered: That's why you're shivering with cold when it's ninety-five degrees in the shade?

I started to get up angrily, but she held me down. She didn't say anything else.

She wiped my brow. Then she leaned over and kissed me.

The taste of her mouth wasn't at all like those of men. It was so gentle that I closed my eyes and savored it like candied papaya. I inhaled it deep into my mouth.

Outside the purview of men, we became happy, playful, for a few minutes. A warm perfume wafted from her navel. We teetered on tiptoes. It was so strange. We were smiling like drowned souls finally at peace. We danced on a tightrope that stretched from her heart to mine.

Finally, we each went our own way home. But I stayed by the window all night, looking her way, wrapped in her jacket as cinnamon-dark as her skin, and I knew she was doing the same.

She never asked questions. What's left of you after all these trades? She knows. There's a metallic sheen that can't be worn away.

Now I hum every time the teacher walks past me. His hand trembles on my notebook. He's so pitiful. He looks like a suicide about to dive. His features are washed out. When he opens his mouth, a croak comes out. He has to clear his throat to be able to talk. The tutoring sessions are a mess. I snigger. He notices.

I laugh because I'm not beautiful in the least. I still don't understand this power I have. My hair is so wild that all my combs break trying to tame it. The combs are afraid of my hair. The rest of me is a plank, with outlines of shapes and occasional curves, but nothing terribly attractive. My features are bunched up in the middle of my face, which is shaped like a triangle. I look like a comic-strip mouse.

Maybe that's why men set traps for me. Maybe that's why I fall into them.

And Troumaron scorches my stomach, my bowels.

At school, they eventually push us out. Or rather, we each fall one by one to the wayside. Most go there just because, to get away from the bitter breath of the neighborhood. Only the smartest and most desperate ones stay.

And I stay. I slip through the net. I won't be held back.

But the struggle to stay wears me out. Ever since the game with the teacher started, I've been feeling tired. He charges for what he knows. He's worse than the others. At least, it's what he wants to do, even if for now, out of hypocrisy or weakness, he isn't able to tell me straight out what he wants. Everything I learn leaves a wound on my body. That knowledge is painful and hard-won.

When the others figure out his game, they shy away from me. It's a joke to them. I'm all alone. Everyone else is an onlooker.

I'm already feeling naked. I shut my eyes and bear it. I play the game. I'll always be the one a man squints at from far off until his hands find me.

Men's hands take hold of you before having even touched you. Once their thoughts turn toward you, they've already possessed you. Saying no is an insult, because you would be taking away what they've already laid claim to.

Like the hand snaking up my T-shirt, they need me to lift my skin so they can feel my organs, or even stop my heart from beating. Their urges won't be constrained. Soon there'll be nothing left to take but they'll keep going anyway.

But why should I let them?

Out of distress. Out of mystery. Confirming angrily, belligerently, hopelessly, what they're all thinking, over there, outside.

Being. Becoming. Not disappearing in your eyes. Escaping the straitjacket of passivity, of idleness, of failure, of ashen gazes, of leaden days, of sharpened hours, of shadowy lives, of faraway deaths, of gravelly failures, of lingering, of nakedness, of ugliness, of mockery, of laughter, of tears, of moments, of eternity, of shortness, of heaviness, of night, of day, of afternoons, of dawns, of faded Madonnas, of vanished temptresses.

None of that is you.

Escaping all that, evading the hunters, the followers, eschewing the path, eluding the dogs, exchanging forms, executing moltings and metaphors and metamorphoses, educing a silvery trail redolent of females and the night's folds, examining the underbrush leading all the way to the depths of myths and exiting anew, skin scoured and with a bloody step out of your lives, being, becoming, not disappearing.

You are not from here, you tell yourself. You repeat that until everything ends.

CLÉLIO

Midnight burns. Noon burns. Every hour burns. Can't keep myself from burning. Have to break something. I'm standing on the building roof, singing at the top of my voice, I sing blues then rap then rock then séga, but the clouds silence my voice, don't care, another song rises to my throat every time, *krapo kriye*, I'm a toad, I yell into the dawn and yell into the dusk and my voice is hoarse from yelling, standing on the roof, I know I'm yelling until I'm strong enough to jump and because the song's saying the mother sleeps with her eyes open and the mother is the father's slave and the father is the boss's slave and the mother therefore is the slave of another slave and it's worse than everything, how can anyone fight for the slave of another slave?

What about me, what am I? I know I'm not a slave, even if a man and a woman among my ancestors were chained up and saw me through the eons separating us, and told me: You will be free. I'm no slave, but maybe everyone else around me is. Putting one foot in front of the other, crossing a threshold, turning their back on things, that's something they can't do. They made their own chains, so they think they're free.

And where would they go if they wanted to move on? To the end of the island, which is the end of the world. We can't leave it. We can't escape it unless we fly. We can't free ourselves unless we die. I'll free all my friends before freeing myself.

You, Carlo, you chose to leave before us all. You say you're in France, you say it's your voice I'm hearing on the phone, but that's not true. I know it. That's not your voice. It's someone fake, trying to pronounce those *r*s but we never say them here. It's someone fake, pretending to be French but you're Mauritian through and through. It's someone fake, yapping about his bottle-green Renault Clio but I know you only like Japanese cars, you swore they were the best cars in the world. It's someone fake who won't answer my questions even though you promised me nothing would drive us apart and you would take me wherever you went.

No, this betrayal has made you someone else. You're not Carlo. I'm taking a knife and carving my leg with your name, Carlo. Now my blood's spelling out your name, you're in me and you are me. There's two of us. The one who talks over there like he's forgotten everything, he's fake.

The toad yells on the roof. It welcomes the night.

It yells, yells, yells. Carlo's blood drips. If I stretch out my arms, will I fly away?

Tell me, since you know.

EVE

He helps me, of course. So it's a trade-off. He gives me books, he pays more attention while correcting my papers. He makes sure, in class, not to look at me more than anyone else, not to ogle me with his milky, wandering eyes, but everybody knows. The smell of a man around the woman he's lusting after doesn't fool anyone. His jerky steps toward her don't, either.

He tells me that he'll tutor me. He tells me to wait after class in the small biology room, since he has a key.

After class, when everybody's left, I stay behind. His searchlight gaze is aimed at me. My eyes burn while I refuse to blink.

His pursuit was ridiculous. It was clear he wasn't used to it. It took him weeks to summon up the courage to tell me to stay after class. He's surprised I say yes so quickly, so coldly. How could it be this easy? He wonders if I really know what his intentions are.

He gives me the key and tells me to go into the room, he'll be there soon. Maybe he's going to regain his courage in the bathroom. Or cool off his burning skin with icy water. Get condoms from his car, I don't know. But I walk into the small room that smells like sulfur and formaldehyde. My steps echo in the hallway lined with vinyl scratched up by thousands of feet. Something flies across the dusty windows. I don't have time to see if it's me.

He's taken care of the setup. The table is at the back of the room, against the wall, in the shadows. We'll sit side by side. I'll be right by the wall. The table's big and solid. And there are also lab benches along the walls. Immediately, the room's function is transformed.

When he comes in and sits down next to me, I see that he

hasn't cleaned up. He's still oozing desire. He stammers nervously. He opens a book at random, tries to discuss something with me. He wants to keep up the masquerade until he's sure I won't run out screaming. He asks me questions and doesn't notice that I'm clearly avoiding direct answers. I just have to smile.

With this smile, he finally seizes the opportunity, turns to me, and holds my face in his hands, his mouth struggles to find mine, he's in such a rush he misses his target.

I love you, I love you, he says, blind with desire. It's so awkward I'm almost insulted. Does he really think I'll believe him? His tongue is in my ear. The words bunch up around the thick mass. That moisture, his hot breath, his fumbling, it all disgusts me. I want to push him away, but I'm up against the wall, his hand's rubbing all over and I hear him whispering, you're not wearing a bra, and then he doesn't say anything at all, he's all hurried and stuck and drowning.

I let him.

He can't even get my clothes off, I have to do it for him. He frees himself and tries to push into me. My head bangs against the wall, but all I feel is tired. He's lost in my body. He's thin in places, flabby in others. I watch him. I notice the bald spot at the top of his head. He's so tall that nobody can see he's losing his hair. I feel like I'm learning things about him that boil down to a few words, things that will destroy him.

The disgust I felt at first has disappeared. Things are boring again. As usual, I don't feel anything anymore. He hammers away. He doesn't come. Do something, he begs. I shrug, then nod.

While he's grabbing my hair, I think to myself how I would have really liked a cigarette.

A cigarette to mask the bitterness in your mouth. Eyes open, you work. Seventeen years old and you dream of nothing. Except continuing to walk beside yourself, fleeing your reflections.

Seventeen years old and you think you know everything. Your face is stony and your hands are exhausted.

EVE

When I walk under the mango trees, they wave to me like they know me. I think I look like lots of things—organic, or mineral, or strange and sloughed-off, but I don't look like a woman. Only a reflection of a woman. Only an echo of a woman. Only the deformed idea of a woman.

In windows, mirrors, eyes, there's my face fleeing endlessly. I don't want my soul trapped in any of those. I'll be anything but a captured soul. But a bird with clipped wings. When I meet my own gaze, I'm chilled and frightened. I hate how much I'm hurting myself.

Someday, tomorrow, later: nothing.

At home, we dance around each other. We're playing a game of avoiding the real questions. They see me and they don't see me. A stench of lies hits me as I walk in the door.

Every day I count my steps before coming back to my place. Or rather, their place, because it isn't mine. I didn't choose to live there. I didn't choose anything at all, even being born. I would have liked an unknown place, with the sea lapping its borders, and a single shapeless filao tree stunted like an old man caught in the wind, and myself sitting under the tree, not doing or saying anything. Sometimes, I'd climb up the highest branches and look into the distance. Far off, there'd be nothing. Except for sea and more sea. The sea's constant, whispering movement. The land would look like it was being rocked to sleep. A moon would slip away. I'd curl up at the bottom of the tree and fall asleep. Maybe I'd never wake up.

There was no fairy at my crib. I think that when I opened my eyes I suddenly saw my whole life in front of me: a stone wall, bars over my eyes, a gag in my mouth, and metal in my heart. That face drove me to pronounce, when I opened my mouth, that vital word: no.

Hide everything and walk on coals, show nothing of myself. I let them think I'm easy come, easy go. I let them think I'm nothing more than a body, this body that, when they pull off its clothes, makes them quiver.

A body so fragile, so thin, so easily broken; a body to cherish and destroy; that's what they try their best to do.

Savita and I have fun dreaming up other selves, born in good places, into families where defeat can't be read in palm lines or bent knees. We'd be doctors or lawyers and we'd care for and defend the weak and the poor. We wouldn't leave anybody to fend for themselves. Those are the stupid dreams we invent for ourselves. But when they become doctors or lawyers, these other girls, do they forget their past? Do they refuse to open the doors they've barricaded?

Savita tickles my toes. I lick the soles of her feet. We have the same skin, completely smooth, into which our hands disappear. The softest parts are the hollows of our backs and the insides of our thighs. When we rub these spots, time stops. I lay my head on her stomach and I hear the sounds of her organs. Something rumbling, some hunger, some urge, I don't know, or maybe it's just her intestines doing their work. We don't really need to talk. We know how to listen to our silences.

SAVITA

Eve's silence is the rumble deep within a volcano. It hurts me to see her so fragile when she thinks she's so strong. When she's serious, her face is like a child's, shocked in a dream, her eyes filled with lights. Her laugh is so rare, but when it comes it's like a hurricane. When I get close to Eve, she sweeps me off my feet.

Before her, I looked at things from so far away that nothing touched me.

I was going to leave that day. I was going to take a little bag and go straight out, walk without looking back. I'd had enough of my parents sniveling. Of all those responsibilities that fell on me as a result, helping my sister, setting a good example for her. We lived in Troumaron as escapees, as refugees among refugees. Living there while insisting on being somewhere else, something else, refusing to accept the signs that we were no different from all the others. At odds with ourselves.

I decided to leave good old Savita, the good girl, behind for good. I didn't know where I'd go. But it wasn't Troumaron I wanted to escape. It was my family. Troumaron was my place, my struggle, my anchor. I'd never experienced anything else. I grew up here. But my parents' eyes saw only another Savita, a sweet girl, a trooper, a winner. I had been forced to fit into that image. I couldn't do it anymore. She wasn't me.

And then, at school, I came across a shipwrecked Eve, her face drowned not in tears but in the shadows of the tree she was sitting under. I saw the walls encircling her. I saw the other schoolchildren's looks, furtive, treacherous. A loneliness so deep it was no different from death.

The most frightening part was that I had the impression she was me.

I went weak. I was riveted by her sadness. Through the opened doors of her sides, her life was escaping. I had to console her, take her in my arms like a mother or a lover, and make her forget, however briefly, why she was shaking.

SAAD

Miracle of my life. The flame trees are in bloom. Thousands of red lips have gorged on the tree, then blossomed all at once. The lychee trees disappear under their fruit. An almost indecent explosion of color, as if shutters have opened onto a body of pure light.

Everywhere I look, the same colors fill my view. My heart sways. Even here, even here, in this city of cement, summer has come. A shrub turns slate blue. The grass becomes momentarily green before yellowing again. On their balconies, women struggle to preserve miniscule blossoms in pots. They no longer feel weighed down in their bodies and so they sing. At night, the smell of fruits can be discerned from that of trash. For a very, very short while, the fruits win out.

Summer numbs us at first, before the heat revives the landfill's call and stirs anew our shadows, our sleepy dregs.

And I, sitting by my window open to everything that could rouse the night, I keep thinking about her. Her eyes' resonance, her body pushing away and feeding fantasies. The kind of body that could completely disappear into your own. That could be eaten. The kind of body that could be folded into all sorts of positions to reach its impossible nooks. And that, from its toes to the end of its hair, would be a place to lose yourself in. Her toes would taste like longan. Her hair would be filled with smells of seaweed and night. Her sex would have the tuberous odor of frangipani flowers and the half-rotten warmth of mangroves.

Oh, I'm off and away, like always. I'm imagining her with someone else, with everyone else. Which makes me even more excited.

I'm jealous, but at the same time, I know I'm the only one to love her. She's waiting for me. I know it. I feel it.

I'm young; take my hand.

Yes, he, the poet, he said that at seventeen, with all too much hope. Too much belief, too much promise. He could write. And then one day, he set aside this too-heavy gift. I want both: to write, and to have Eve. Eve and writing. Hand in hand. Having only one of them is as good as nothing. They are the fruits that will sate me, the seeds that will sprout more plants and multiply my voice like a banyan tree swallowing up land.

I know that, for now, I can't create anything. I can only copy. My voice isn't my own. This language isn't my own. I don't even know who I'm talking to.

But this room will end up becoming something real. I reread madness on the walls, in black and white ink, and I tell myself that I'm also in the process of creating, even if it's with other people's words. I was a child who stumbled over words. I'll become a man who tames them. Of course, the day they open the door, they won't understand anything, they won't know what's being hammered and chiseled here. But having done that reassures me. I've performed that act. I don't know what it's worth, but I've done something. I haven't just stayed here and faded away into death. I'm inscribing myself, rather than erasing myself. I've built a bridge with a child who's also angry at heart, even if he'll never know me. He tells me:

The star wept rose into the heart of your ears, an infinity of white rolled between your nape and hips and man bled black onto your sovereign side.

I'm young; take my hand.

I love a girl whose body has been crushed. But the day I'm in her, I'll wipe all the marks off her body; she'll be new.

I'm young; I'm in love.

The sun's gotten into my body. It's the core of what I'm writing. A portrait of Eve in the echoes of my room. Sentences that describe her, that draw her out. I'm in love.

I believe in possibilities. Yes, even here. Even hurtling down our slopes. A word described her for me that day when we raced downward on bikes from the Virgin Mary. That day, right when she told me she would never say I love you, I saw the word that described her, a word at once resonant and foreign in this place: grace. If this grace is part of my possibilities, I thought, I can do anything.

Port Louis looks at me differently. I believed dark, ugly Port Louis, disfigured by grotesque shapes, insurmountable in its waves of humankind, was beckoning to me. Its black pigeons dotting every roof agreed to decipher its moods for me. The city told me: if there are moments like this one and faces like your own, then, you have to love me, if only for this.

I know this, that I'm only a simulacrum. But a drop of blue ink has gotten into me. I transform it into a black child's ink, lacerating the walls. This story you're reading on my walls, its words will only disappear when the buildings born out of the cyclones' waters have disappeared.

Sometimes, when the wind comes from Signal Mountain, when I see the fires burning on its slopes, the scrub fires, the trash fires,

I tell myself that under all that is beauty, even here, and something is sizzling, and a fire is sparking in the underbrush of my own mind.

I forget what I am, where I come from. The wind from the mountain erases the name Troumaron from my lips and from my memory.

I want to leave and I want to stay. Between the two, I do not move. But my body cannot stop wandering over our pool of dreams, at Eve's mercy.

CLÉLIO

The factory smells like engine grease, decaying waste, abandoned sandals, wasted bodies. Sometimes I come here all alone so I can see how life tells lies to the poor. Does me good. My mother, when she got a job here, she thought everything had changed. She took her first paycheck and bought me Nike shoes, she thought that would make me happy, she never saw that I was sick of Nikes, that we had all these tricks for getting these pointless things, I didn't need things, I needed a guide, I needed purpose.

After that, she changed, from one week to the next. The factory grew and got deep into our lives. My mother started bringing me defective sweaters. If I see another Ralph Lauren sweater with one sleeve shorter than the other I'll cut it up and stuff it down the mouth of this man who made lopsided beings of us. But for us, it's not sleeves. It's arms, or legs, or eyes that are uneven. We're defective humans.

She got smaller, grayer. She got less and less sunlight. At the end of the day, when she came back in, she was like a blurred copy of herself. Something had started rubbing away at her features. My father sat in a chair waiting for her. He spent his day waiting for her, like an old idiot, his eyes like a lost kid's, but all he could say when she got home was, Did you bring something to eat? He didn't bother to say anything else. Every time he said that I wanted to wring his neck. Let her sit down, take off her shoes, drink a glass of water, you shithead, I wanted to yell at him, go make your dinner yourself. Or tell her you spent all day in front of the window watching for her shadow.

She had rings under her eyes as deep as Père Laval's grave, her eyes were sunk that deep. Her hair had started falling out. It was like strings. I don't think she ate enough. Her hands look like the moon with so many craters.

Then they brought in Chinese workers who worked fast and good and without complaining. Or maybe they were complaining in their own language and nobody could understand them. They told the Mauritians they had to do the same if they wanted to keep their job. Some of them were fired. But my mother worked hard. She wasn't a loser. She was a fighter, like me. Well, not exactly, but more or less. It didn't matter. She was fired when the factory closed since it cost too much to make sweaters and shirts here. My father said that between the American and Chinese giants our country was an ant that nobody noticed, even when stepping on us. Would you even think twice before crushing an ant? he asked. It's all the same to them. It's not injustice, it's just economic rationale.

Sometimes my father isn't as stupid as he appears to be.

I'd have really liked it if Carlo sent us a little money, helped us, even if he didn't want to come back. But he still hasn't sent anything. He calls Mam, and her face lights up like a Christmas tree. It gets me so mad, Mam being excited for fake Carlo, believing all his lies, telling me, *li pu fer mwa vinn kot li en Frans, li ena enn zoli lakaz ek dis lasam*, yeah, I've never heard any Troumaron guys talking about having a ten-room house in France and promising their mothers for ten years that they'll bring them there and then not doing it.

Carlo, it's over. I'm done with the fake you. The real one's right here by me. We'll sit on the roof and laugh, we'll tell stories, like before, he's my big brother, as handsome as a god and when he's here I'm not afraid of anything.

Tonight I have my guitar with me. I lie down as the last bit of sun stains my head and set my guitar on my belly, I play it easy. Going to sing songs I've been thinking up, songs I'm not singing for anyone else. Carlo would understand if he was here.

Ki to pe atann? Personn. Ki lavi finn donn twa? Nayen. Komye dimunn inn fer twa promes? Zot tu. Komye dimunn inn gard zot parol? Okenn. Dimunn pa gard parol, zot zis kass to leker, pa bizin per, fer kuma zot, kas zot leker, pas to simin, pa krwar nayen. Pa krwar nayen, to pa pu sufer. Pa krwar nayen to pa pu sufer.

I don't believe in anything. But I suffer all the same.

SAVITA

After school she tells me, I have to go. I try to convince her to stay, but she disappears into herself, like she always does just when I've gone a bit too far.

Inflexible Eve, that's what I call her.

I've gone with you so many times. I've taken you to your place so many times. It's like I'm always there at the right moment to pick you up. But it's because I always listen for you. You never call. But I hear you anyway.

But watching you run away like this, I feel sad. You could say no if you wanted to. Why do you have to give yourself up to them? Why do you always bind yourself to them? I don't understand.

I want to protect you. I want to keep you from losing yourself. I want to be the one who saves you from yourself.

Sometimes your voice breaks; sometimes my heart breaks just seeing you. Neither of us is innocent, and I hate the world for it.

I'd give my life for you.

It seems so easy. Only you would know what I mean. All the beauty and pain that those words carry.

Sitting on the balcony, I look your way. Here, nothing belongs to me except for you. I hear my father's impatience as he waits for the treasure chest to open for him. I hear my mother's incredulity as she listens to him daydreaming and sneers at him. I try to listen to myself, but all I can hear is the air going in and out of my lungs. The body's automatism. And the lack of life.

My little bag stays in my closet, still full, still waiting for my decision to leave.

The smell of food makes me think that you are hungry but do not know it, you who only nibble on bitter fruit.

Don't you think my face is shaped like a mouse's? you asked me one day.

I kiss your mouse-shaped face. You're the world's beauty, its light.

EVE

The sea surges, escapes, scatters. It moves a thousand memories and a thousand scraps. Papers, cans, broken glass, smells of death. The neighborhood's life is dragged away by stream waters, swelling and bursting its banks.

I wait for the stream to subside so I can go back. I don't want to see anyone. I wait for night to fall and cover everything, including the shapes of people nearby and even the shapes of things.

The other day, in the office I'd been called to, I looked at the city and I saw it as it had been that morning with Saad at the statue of the Virgin Mary. Pale and sleepy. From high up, everything was smoothed out. The sharp edges were worn down, the holes filled in. The air-conditioned office, cushioned with carpets, smelled like new leather. You wanted to snuggle up in the armchairs. There was a huge painting reflected in the window. It winked at me. I recognized it. A teacher had told us about the artist, Malcolm de Chazal. I could see within his potbellied dodos and cheerful flowers those childhood dreams that had long since been forgotten.

I could have slept here, sheltered, in this bubble at a remove from reality. I could have slept in the foreign leather and the hissing air conditioner and the smooth, monotonous light. I could have slept in this white place, where I would have been protected from sunlight and screaming. In this twilight, not of the day but of the senses, I feel all right. But I know that if I slept there I would wake up with my heart frozen. My body numb from the lifelessness. Maybe that's what the man drinking one glass of whiskey after another on the other side of the desk is trying to exorcise through

63

me. He needs a body to thaw himself in. He needs a life to make himself feel alive. I understand him: he struggled for so long to get here and now that he's here, he doesn't know what he wants anymore. He's made a life, but not a home.

He looks at the girl with childlike eyes, standing in front of the window. I'm not in a rush. I wait. I look. I'd look all night, if he left me here. The city, the night, the void.

What you're looking for isn't here, I wanted to tell him. But I can hear him replying: Nor is what you're looking for, either.

You're calm. Your hair makes black splashes. Your face is serious. He's heard about you. He's been told, she's not like the others. He sees that it's true. He's been told, she does everything. He doesn't know if it's true. You don't ask for anything. You're stern and bewitching, that's what he thinks of you. But they also told him what they did to you. Parties where you were alone and they were many. How one morning they left you almost lifeless not far from your neighborhood.

It's not hard for him to imagine it. Your bones are so thin.

What do you want? What are you looking for?

At that moment, you turn around and he gets up, unbuckling the belt of his pants.

EVE

The stream quiets down. I do, too. One day, I was left here by men who had gone crazy, drinking from my body. They hadn't taken me to an air-conditioned office but to an island right by the island, an island full of winds, birds, scrub, and snakes.

They got drunk and the moon got into their heads. They did some kind of dance around me, they pulled off their clothes, they looked like heavy, clumsy birds on their tiny feet. When they pounced on me, I saw that I was something foreign to them. We destroy what's foreign to us. Then we gather it up like a bag of sand in a boat where the water washes it.

I wake up as that bag of sand, I look at the sky thick with stars, and I tell myself: This is the last time.

But the men hunt me down and life goes on and I'm so indifferent to myself that I don't resist.

I'm trying to figure out where life's limit must be. What color it would be. What exactly the point of no return would be, that would tell me what I am.

I keep walking forward. One step after another, but it's always the same step, repeated endlessly. Step after step in the same place, the only aim being to contradict itself.

My feet take me past other girls, other women, other boys, other men. Some rush ahead, their heads bent down. Others fall back. All of them vanish into the distance, leaving me alone.

My body is crushed by waves in all directions, by a tumult of winds.

They run to escape, swallowing the harshness of their future. I stay afloat.

By the open window, nobody answers me. I would have liked to know what was watching out for me, what was driving me. The root of this refusal. What planted this negation in me.

The school principal told me: *Vous vous devez de réussir.* Then she said it again in English: You owe it to yourself to succeed. And, finally, in Mauritian Creole: *Pa gaspiy u lavi.* In three languages, she told me the same thing. That I'm responsible. I have to forget the place I go back to each night, how the cockroaches follow the same path as me, how this path is littered with cripples. Parts of bodies, arms, legs, eyes. People reduced to their most invisible selves. Along my path curious, hazy eyes follow me and seem to ask me, who are you, walking with such aimless eyes?

They don't understand me, these people unused to life who slip and disappear through the neighborhood's cracks.

Trash hammers the road like shrapnel. The ruts seem dug by mortar fire. On TV faces are talking about war. But here, I feel like I'm living through a siege. We're at war, yes, against ourselves and against these bodies growing on us like parasites.

But this isn't just the city. The world is also fighting against everything that staggers forward, everything that doesn't walk in victory. Its distant rhythms aren't for us. It's better to be born blind so as not to see the rage in its eyes. Everybody's preparing for war. We're all born with this naked and open flesh. Then each of us fashions an armor of thorns and spiky brambles. But the two sexes don't have the same heritage. We're not born with the same burdens.

What do men give in exchange for a body? They don't give their own body; a man has to take. They protect themselves. They watch their shadows. We're butterflies caught in a net, even at our most exultant, even at our most resistant. We're stolen bodies.

The days follow one another. Savita tries to hold me back, to intertwine with me, to save me from myself, but it's too late. She's already like a happy memory. I know that she won't follow me where I'm going.

When I tell her I'm staying at school after class, she looks at me and doesn't reply. Her heart, weighed down with everything she can't say, giving out.

One day she told me, I'm waiting for you.

And since then, every time, she's waited for me, like she's waiting for me tonight.

SAAD

They slip between the walls like two little ghosts laughing at us. They dance in front of everyone as if nobody would notice them at all. They almost seem like two virgins, these two little ones, if their movements didn't have this slowness suggestive of night rather than day. I would have seen them as vestals if they had made me the object of their worship. All dressed in white, their veils barely hiding their gentle hearts, their swaying hips, their bronze backsides.

But they're like two hands on a body. They don't need a third. They are free to do whatever they like, whenever they like. Their smiles suggest no need for any boys. Their eyes bind them to each other. We are invisible.

That scares the gang. I can sense something changing in them, even after they've tolerated Eve's escapades for so long, and Savita's distant prettiness, and even what drew them together at first. But they don't want these female bodies being dangled in front of them with no hope of a taste. Eve can move from man to man, but when she's with Savita, that's when she slips away. We're not yours, the two of them say. We never will be. On their tiptoes they slip and slide. The cigarettes flare with sharp inhalations and reveal malicious glimmers in the guys' eyes. Kenny whispers, it's time to teach those two a real lesson. The others just get hard. Yeah, what's their game? A girls' game, sure, but no way these sluts have any idea what's coming to them.

And they keep talking.

I try my best to calm them down, to change their mind. I have to think up a hundred different ways to distract them. I say to Clélio, hey Clélio, remember that car you got the license plate number for, yeah, I have the address, my uncle handles vehicle registration stuff. But Clélio's in his own little world, he's biting his nails to the quick, and when that happens he doesn't have any time to listen to me. But everyone else is all for it: let's go slash the tires on that huge four-by-four, they say. Let's break the windows and give that little lady a scare.

Nobody really wants to go do it, but when you're a gang, you have to forget that you're a person, you have to be part of this moving, powerful, hot body that nothing can stop. Once you start moving, you have to go all the way.

Clélio doesn't want to come.

Leave him, says Kenny, he's got his head in the clouds.

We can't leave him alone, I say.

Leave me alone, says Clélio, as he's peeling away the dead skin on his soles.

And I do it, because I want to get the rest of them away from Savita and Eve. I want to distract them from the two women.

We leave the *cité* at the mercy of Clélio's breakneck fury.

EVE

Savita's just left me in front of my place. I didn't go inside right away, as usual. Tonight, more than ever, everything's weighing down on me. The teacher's thrown me off. He was like a lizard; he seemed to actually be in love with me—as much as a man can actually know how to love. He stares at me for minutes on end and sighs, and then, suddenly, he unleashes a pent-up fury, but that doesn't even make me angry.

Tonight, something weird happened. Something I'd never experienced before.

Just when he realized it, he seemed shaken, as if he was about to start crying. I can't figure it out. I don't think he just wants my body, the way everyone else does. I think he wants me, too, the soft and warm thing beneath my icy crust. When he puts his hands in me, I feel like he's trying to find that. To find me right where it hurts so much to be touched. But maybe he's just like all the others and wants to see me wince in pain, and that's all it is. Maybe he's just a man the same way all the others are men.

Fortunately, Savita waits for me every time in front of the school. When I see her, I forget what's just happened. When I see her, I catch a glimpse of the moments to come and I can shut the door on what tears me apart.

I think of Savita tonight, she who saves me from myself.

SAVITA

I'm afraid tonight. I'm walking her home again, but after what I've seen, I can't stop shaking. But she seems so calm, so distant from everything, even though her thighs are red.

I feel weak and dizzy. I have trouble walking. The air is heavy. It's so hot my body is sweating. I'm not the one holding her up anymore, she's the one guiding me. I'm thinking again about what I saw in the classroom. I didn't want to look. But she was late coming out, so I thought maybe she'd already left. I went up. The door wasn't completely shut.

I think he saw me, or smelled me. Not her. She was forgotten. I ran out. I went back down to wait for her. When she came, I could see in her eyes that she didn't know I'd seen her. She took me by the arms, as usual. I looked up. Someone was looking at us from above. That gaze bored into me. I felt its bite.

I started walking fast, but my feet were so heavy. She heard me gasping, and she said, what's wrong? But as usual, those nights, she was only half there. The other half was somewhere else. The other half tried to come back and disappear within herself.

I have to talk to her. We need to leave, to escape. The guys from the neighborhood are becoming men, with all their hatred. Soon they'll take it out on us. They can't bear to see us together, just the two of us. She doesn't pay attention to them. But I do. I see the anger growing in them. I see the heat rising in their thoughts. We have to leave.

But how can I run away when I feel so heavy? I have trouble walking. I have trouble breathing. The ground is stuck to my feet.

My feet are sinking in lava. Soon I won't be able to move anymore. The volcano will tear me to pieces.

Promise me you'll gather up my pieces, Eve, I say.

What are you saying? she asks.

I don't know.

She hugs me close.

My darling Savita, she says, I won't just gather up your pieces, I'll eat them so you'll always be in me.

I tried to joke: I always knew you were a cannibal!

She bit my shoulder lightly. I wanted her to leave teeth marks on my skin. That would be my only souvenir of her.

As we each went our way, I realized that I was crying, without really knowing why. Our apartments aren't far apart. I left her in front of her building. I just have to walk past where all the trash is, and I'll be at my place. But in the darkness, it feels like such a long way to go. As long as life itself.

PART TWO

SAAD

Last night was perfectly ordinary. Last night was another life. And then, in the morning, this. Nobody understands what's happened. Even in Troumaron, this has never happened, certainly not ever like this. The neighborhood is quieter than it's ever been. Everybody's hiding. Nobody dares to say that it had to happen at some point. We don't want to believe that about ourselves.

She was found in the trash, at the bottom of a trash bin.

Nobody heard anything. Everybody was looking the other way, of course. Ignorance is our only protection.

We, the boys, even if we'd known something, we wouldn't have said a thing. We don't snitch.

We know that some of us are monsters hidden behind ordinary appearances. That our seeming banality can mask murderous eyes. It's a legacy of childhood, this brutality, but it never comes fully to the fore. Usually it's the quietest ones, the sleepiest ones. Their eyelids seem so heavy. We can't see how their eyes are bloodshot. Something hazy clouds their decay. But most of us are normal kids. We play at being terrors, but deep down we're not doing anything really terrible. At some point we'll fall into line again, after feeling like we've had some freedom to be ourselves. So we don't understand.

What happened? Nobody had anything against her, Savita.

I think of the last line I wrote on the walls, last night: Your mouth in red memory opens for the sovereign man's blood.

I was riffing on Rimbaud, as usual. But it's true: man is sovereign. He will be until the planet changes its orbit.

When I see Eve again, I'm paralyzed by her face. She's gone completely blank. Obliterated.

Now I understand why she couldn't say I love you to a man.

Bloodless, bent over, broken down. She's sitting by the stream. She's not crying. She's curled up into herself like an egg in its shell. She's chewing over her grief. She's trying to spit it out, but it's stuck in her mouth, in her throat. She retches but nothing comes out, not the least drop of deliverance. I can't even try to touch her. She's so far gone.

I can only sit by her and watch her shaking. As the day goes by and the shaking doesn't stop, I see her drifting away into her memories, disappearing into her loss. She's lost. Eve will never be mine. I'll never stop loving her. But I, too, feel a sort of death. I will never be the same Saad. I didn't understand sadness until this day.

Off in the distance police cars are coming. There's noise in the neighborhood. The guys would rather hide. But the police change everything.

I take her balled-up fists and open them up. Her hand is studded with small red crescents, as if the new moon had trampled over it. I bring my lips to those red crescents. She pulls away her hands. She wants to hurt herself. She wants to cry. But she can't.

Talk to me, I say to her.

I saw her last night, right before, she says.

We said good-bye a few feet away from there, from where.

I didn't go inside. I could have followed her, held onto her a little longer, been with her.

But I came here, to the stream. I was here and I didn't see anything.

I didn't see anything.

I was the last one. I could have. If I had. I should have. Why. If. But. Instead. She. And then.

She finally curls up into herself with a creak like an axletree. She pounds her fists against the ground. She pounds so hard that the earth squelches all around. She gets up and begins punching her fists in every direction, narrowly missing me. I get up and grab her. After a minute she calms down, even if her voice keeps lashing out.

She asks me:

Who did it?

I don't know. I have no idea.

That's impossible, she says. You're everywhere, you hear everything, you know everything. It was one of the guys from the gang who did it. You know it and you're not going to say anything, because you're all watching out for each other.

That's not true. Eve, I swear to you we weren't there last night.

Where were you?

On a drive. We weren't doing anything in particular. We were just looking for guys to scare.

She imitates me unkindly: We were just looking for guys to scare. You sure you weren't looking for someone to kill, too?

She's standing and looking at me with so much contempt that I don't know where to start.

You wrote "sovereign man," she says. They're sovereigns for you, too. You don't dare to stand up to them. You'd never dare to tell on them. You have to fit in, no matter what. You're a coward and a show-off and a liar. Pitiful.

She runs off without waiting for any other explanation. But

I didn't lie. I might be a coward, but I'm not a liar. And she doesn't know that I'm protecting her from the wolves.

And then I start tearing up the ground myself, but nobody sees me. I'm the only one who knows what's twisting in my stomach.

EVE

The body is lying naked on the bench, like it's ready to be cut up. But this isn't an autopsy.

Lying, naked, on a bench in the biology room, I try to imagine myself wherever Savita is, spread out under the gazes of policemen and doctors, waiting to figure out her secrets. Waiting to splatter red on the white earthenware. But no, a dead body doesn't splatter. Only a living body gushes red.

Saadiq wrote, on the wall: Your mouth in red memory opens for the sovereign man's blood.

What did she, Savita, get from the sovereign man? Punches. Cuts. And maybe something else.

And for me, it's not blood I'll be getting, but a male's sperm that invades and drowns the female, that disperses within her millions of his potential doubles.

But I'll never carry his doubles. My body won't be colonized.

My body is lying, naked, on the table.

A thin body to treasure or tear apart, they say.

And right now he is treasuring me and tearing me apart at the same time. He struggles and staggers under the force of his urges. I have never seen him so destroyed. His shadow on the wall is gigantic. That of a monstrous creature overlooking me. It doesn't look like anything human, this stooped, wavering shadow emitting guttural, sucking sounds, the sounds of inhuman suffering.

Why did I come tonight? After what happened to Savita? I don't belong here. But I don't belong anywhere. I can't mourn Savita in my home, or in hers.

So I do it here, with all the force of my hatred. I hate your death, Savita, and I hate this man who relieves himself in me without caring about whether I'm alive or dead.

Afterward, when he's done slobbering, I'll get up and, the better to destroy him, sit on this table to do my work in the silence of the room, in the bodily smells all around, my clothes rumpled, my hair still wet, my mouth dry, my body emptied out, my soul worn out, my memories dirtied, my days paid for, my pride ripped open, my sex loosened, and the letters and words of my knowledge like lead on the page but still meaningless, without any illumination, displaying their powerlessness and indifference because Savita will not be out there waiting for me like always to tie the rope of my life together again within my body and without that, I don't have any life, anything to hold me up over the emptiness, anything to keep me from letting go.

Like her. But she never let go. Someone else did it for her. Someone thought she wasn't worth any more than the trash he threw her into.

As he's leaving, he says: What about this girl they found dead in Troumaron?

I wait a minute, and then I answer: I knew her.

I see the other question flickering on his lips, which he does not dare to pronounce. I answer it anyway: You did, too.

I know that when I leave, he'll stay at the window, in the darkness, he'll see me disappear in the schoolyard. He'll wonder whether he'll see me tomorrow. Or, as I head home in the dark, alone, whether I'll see the light of day tomorrow.

The street is etched by car headlights, by indifferent traffic. What about him? Is he indifferent to what's happened? Would he caress me as if I was a dead body, too, on the autopsy table? What difference would there be?

On the bench in the biology room, he dissected a human body, nothing more, nothing less.

CLÉLIO

The city's swarming with suits.

Nobody likes that. We feel uncomfortable, even if we haven't done anything wrong. We're not cut out for suits.

I feel like everyone's looking at me funny. My mother starts crying like a Madonna as soon as she sees me. My father is like a live wire. But I haven't done anything. I'm not guilty. If I wanted to murder kids, I wouldn't pick the ones who couldn't defend themselves. I'd pick the ones hurting the others.

The sky's heavy. The wind prowls low. Everybody in the gang's hiding from me. I don't get why. I didn't go with them last night, but that's no reason to be pissed off.

They're all cowards. I try to sing, but anger swallows up my voice the minute it comes out. I'm not singing to feel happy, I'm singing to talk to Savita. Of course nobody understands it. They don't understand that it's possible to talk to shadows more alive than themselves.

Everywhere I turn, there are policemen. The trash bin is the center of their anthill. Do they actually think they'll find something here besides a girl's corpse? You think that an angel will come down to Troumaron to show them the way? No, all there is here is death. If they're astonished when death comes, it's because they didn't want to see anything. But I've got my eyes open. I know death will come and claim every one of us, in the worst way possible. That's why I've begun practicing.

EVE

The apartment smells like sulfur. As soon as I walk in, it begins burning.

They're waiting in the living room covered with calendar pictures. They ask the usual questions, edged with fear. I answer evasively. Then I figure it out. Savita's death has changed everything. Her parents have been openly saying what they've been thinking: that I dragged her down into the pit. If she's dead, it's my fault, they say.

My father asks me: Do you know anything about her death?

I would have liked to say, I'm not guilty, but I can't. Because I was her, because she was me, I'm guilty. We both died at the same moment. All that's left of me is useless. The words lodge in my mouth. The taste of my saliva nauseates me.

My father says: They said you set a bad example for her.

I answer: Do you know any good examples around here?

He immediately gets up and slaps my face. I was expecting it, of course. He has no other answer to my words. He has no other response to my presence. I moved as he slapped me, and the strike wasn't nearly so strong.

My mother has been reduced to almost nothing: a larva of a mother. I get up, tired. I don't care about them. I don't want to see them. They don't know anything about her. They don't have any imagination. How could they know what she lived through? She doesn't matter to them. All that matters is what people think, what people say, it's about appearances, the whole façade of normalcy, their pitiful pride. Their pride? There's nothing to boast about here. Their mouths are thick with the sludge of mudslinging.

Leave me the fuck alone, I say.

All I can think about is lying in Savita's calm sunlight.

But he sees I'm tired and punches me, a solid fist punch to my face. I fall onto the armchair in shock. My mother cries out.

He grabs my hair and forces me to look and listen to him. I shut my eyes and cover my ears.

He yells curses. He lashes out in such a red rage that even our neighbors and their own neighbors can hear him. His fury echoes further and further, like the aftershocks of an earthquake.

I'm not really paying attention to what he's saying anymore. He yells at my mother while he's still holding me by my hair. I wait, patiently, for him to stop.

The only thing I tell myself is that I need to think about cutting my hair. Cut it short, very short. Shave it until my skull can be seen. I'll go bareheaded. Like a lioness nobody would dare touch or even look at directly. Touch a lioness and lose a hand. Teeth sinking into skin, sharp and heavy teeth, teeth thick with blood. And then, digesting in the sun, the lioness will lick them gently to wash them. A lioness's breath is thick and bloody. The beauty of a lioness digesting, golden and luxuriant.

Finally, noticing my absent gaze, he yanks his hands out of my hair, pulling out several tufts as well.

I go into my room at last. I spit bitter saliva. I throw myself onto my bed, paying no attention to the pain in my scalp. Everything I might ever suffer is nothing compared to what Savita endured.

She was stripped of her body and her life by the sovereign man.

He refused her any dignity and threw her into a trash bin. He decreed: You are nothing. You don't exist. You've lived for nothing.

You're not useful for anything. You're over.

The man, in his uselessness, prevails. What does she say? What does she do? Does she cry? Does she accept the inevitable? Is she happy that she's been finished off? Does she think of me in her final moments? Does she ask me, why aren't you there?

On a table, somewhere, under a harsh light, her body waits to be decoded. To reveal what? Signs of death? There's no need to open her up to figure that out. Remnants, traces, incriminating liquids? And what about me? Will they find traces of me on her, traces of my hands, my lips, my pleasure? What will the autopsy say about her? Be your silence, Savita. They don't deserve anything more.

Outside, electricity crackles. More than Savita's death, the police presence strips bare the cables of tension crisscrossing the city. I feel like, now that she's left, I'm the only one facing the horde. Everybody's looking right at me. As if I'd broken the laws. I had disturbed the pattern, changed the space, broken open the locked doors. I sow discord. I give off a smell of greasy soot. I'm the fallen angel of the neighborhood, its ripped-out soul.

I'm so convinced of it that I start to doze off in exhaustion.

I grab the edge of a sheet and pull it over my face like a shroud. My body is so flat it's barely an eddy in the small ocean of the bed. My eyes are open beneath the shroud. I try to see the world through this soft grille, this mesh. What would I do if I had to hide from everybody? How would I live as a ghost? Or does invisibility free us from our fears?

I slip into a half-sleep under my shroud, looking at a white world. Soon, everything slackens. Even my breath, the rhythm of a broken pendulum, subsides.

CLÉLIO

There was no getting away from it. I was the first one to be questioned. The first suspect. Nobody said anything, of course. But there are plenty of ways to say something without saying anything. The old guys are just waiting for that. These kids are more or less okay, they say, but, sure, there's a couple of bad apples in there. One of them's been in prison, he's always looking for trouble. You know, if their hearts are black, there's nothing you can do. *Ki pu fer, ena, zott finn ne kum sa.* That's just how they were born, rotten to the core.

Fuck it, I'm not that shitty! Those men are the shitheads. Nobody says my name, but I feel like I'm hearing it everywhere, in the air, in the church bells tolling Sunday Mass, in the car tires screeching. Even my first name doesn't come out right when anyone says it. But the policemen aren't all idiots. They're doing their job. If one of us has been in prison, that simplifies things. What were you doing last night? Last night? Nothing. Nothing? Nothing at all. You didn't have anything to do? No, there are times when I don't do anything. Where were you? On my apartment roof. Who saw you? Well, the birds flying over my head, I don't know if they were finches or cape canaries or cardinals, and then there are bats flying around as soon as it's dark out. Stop messing with us!

If they're looking for proof, they'll find it in their little folders. Your honor, this boy is a repeat offender. Society has done all it can to rehabilitate him, but there are people who just can't be redeemed, Your honor, and the judge will look at me solemnly and he will ask, in English, Are you beyond redemption? as if he were asking that question of himself, but I'll tell him, *Oui, je suis au-delà de la rédemption*, because I don't want to be redeemed or rehabilitated, and I haven't committed the crimes you're imputing to me, as they say in their legal jargon, I haven't done anything at all, other people committed the worst crimes, but the police won't dare to arrest these guys, or if they have to, it'll be with velvet gloves and they'll say excuse me, Monsieur, before locking them up and they won't lay hands on those guys, they'll smell as crisp and fresh as the millions of rupees they've laundered and just as unattainable, which will make these poor officers with their crappy salaries dream, you've got to understand them, there are things that go beyond poor people's imaginations but okay, they still have to be arrested because that's how it is, the people need to be shown that there will be justice even if they're released the same night and their trials don't go anywhere because they have to shut up all the activists whining about corruption in this country and slush funds and liquidated assets, and so I'm beyond redemption, and you can pin that murder on me without even saying please or showing any actual proof, I'm guilty of being me, I'm guilty of just being, and they'll shove me, and hit the back of my head and say, you have to talk, you little pimp, and if they have to they'll beat me up without leaving any signs, and then it'll turn into a story of race and communities, it's always like that, even if Savita, she joked about these things, when she died she became a racial symbol, and now I am, too, over the centuries we've been enemies, slaves, coolies, it's a nasty history, for sure, which is why it keeps happening again and again, it's been going on for centuries now and it's not going to end anytime soon, believe me, even if we the children of Troumaron don't care about religion, race, color, caste, everything that divides all the other guys on this shitty island, we the children of Troumaron, we're a single community, and it's a universal one, this community of the poor and the lost and that, believe me, is the only identity that counts.

I'm leaving this place with handcuffs on my wrists. There's no way out.

SAAD

They took Clélio away. I knew we shouldn't have left him alone. Whenever he's on his own, he gets into trouble. I know he didn't kill Savita. But he's the Perp. They'll try to make him say it and even if they can't do it, it won't make a difference. Clélio just has to open his mouth and he'll be sentenced. He's stupidly, totally innocent.

In the meantime, she, Eve, has a new obsession: she wants to see Savita's body. I don't know what she's hoping for, but I keep trying not to help her and she keeps pushing me to. But she's started talking to me again, and that's something at least. It's better than a poke in the eye with a blunt stick. I have some hope again. I take her to the police headquarters.

The officers look at us indifferently at first, then, once they hear where we're from, suspiciously. Especially me. They take more kindly to her, she looks so young with her big T-shirt and her hair pulled back in a ponytail, yes, she seems really young, like she's fifteen years old. And then there's that dark splotch on her right cheek, isn't that a typical feature, isn't that the mark of life in those tormented places?

The officers buzz around her like fat bumblebees.

The inspector takes us into his office. He remains standing. He's huge and seems fatherly, but I don't entirely trust him. He touches her face, strokes the swelling there with his thumb, a thick brown thumb on this small face, I want to slap it and I can see in the way he's looking at me that he knows it.

Did your boyfriend do this to you? he asks.

My father, she says as she looks right into his eyes.

He lets his hand drop. She sizes him up. She asks what she has to do for him to let her see the body. They consider each other. I have no part to play here. There's a coded conversation in their silence.

She's in the morgue, he says.

So, is it far away? The morgue? she asks.

Why would you want to see her?

She was my friend.

We only let close family see the body.

I'm family.

We'll return it to you when the autopsy's done. It's best to wait.

He goes back to his paperwork with an air of finality.

I drag her out of the headquarters before she tries to do something else. I don't understand this ease she has in paying for things with her body. As if it didn't mean a thing. I think it's the most precious thing in the world.

I take her to the Caudan waterfront because I know she doesn't want to go back to Troumaron. She's devastated. We sit and look at the sea and wait. The bruise on her face has turned purple under the streetlights. It actually looks beautiful.

The sea by the luxury hotel gleams with hazy fire. Where we live, it looks like oil and smells like an armpit.

People walk past, sit at a café, take in the air, drink beers, enjoy the weather, and think about nothing. Eve once told me that we were on another planet. I think she's right. Our sun and theirs aren't the same.

She doesn't say anything. She doesn't see anything. She isn't there.

How can I reach her?

We walk on glass parapets, over the clear void. There are a thousand silences between us and all the distance of infinity.

I light a joint for her. She inhales sharply and her eyes turn to warm honey. Their colors mass on my tongue like the honey of voracious flowers from Rodrigues. *To lizie kuma dimiel Rodrig,* I say to her in my head. The ganja races through my body, shimmers in my veins. My words are simple and straightforward.

We'll get through this, I tell her.

Maybe you will. Not me. I don't have any energy. It's all gone.

But there are options. Pretending, persuading, that's what will help us get out.

She smiles.

Your words, she says, you borrow them from other people, and they'll help you fool people. Yes, you'll get out.

It upsets me to hear her say that.

If I use them, I say, then they're mine. I take them. Words don't belong to anyone.

And they belong to everyone. You're free to do whatever you want. I won't follow you. It's too late.

How can it be too late when you're seventeen?

I feel old, she says.

We're practically children, sitting on our parapet. And she, with that flower of violence on her cheek, feels old. She gets up and walks a few steps in front of me. She seems completely off-balance. She's dancing and falling at the same time. I hold out my hand to catch her.

Did this place make us this way, or is it the other way around?

I don't answer. In my head, I make her a promise: Eve, I will bring you out of your ruins.

Smoking together, we're closer than we've ever been. She lays her head on my shoulder. I'm filled with the herbal smell of the joint, but even more so with the smell of her. Her skin and flesh. I smell her sweat. I smell her hair. I smell something else, something secret, urgent, living, something buried, something so intensely feminine that, even in my sleepiness, I'm dizzy with desire. I pull her up against me. Oh, how I want you! I tell her without daring to say it out loud. How I want you!

EVE

Other kinds of graffiti have replaced Saadiq's phrases and the older curses. On our floor, it's an explosion of hatred. The fecal taste of it all stays in my mouth.

My father's fury hasn't subsided. Suddenly, he's playing the perfect role. He's not the father who beats his daughter, but the father who "corrects" his daughter. That makes all the difference. I have to sneak out when there are fewer people outside. I avoid everybody's gaze so as not to feel their intensity on my skin.

My father has long conversations with the other men in the building. When he comes back, he reeks of the local wine. My mother withdraws into herself like a turtle. That's what "till death do us part" means.

At school, I do nothing. There's nothing left for me to do now. Some teachers try to talk to me, but they give up when they see my deadened eyes. The other teacher tries to get close to me again, he slips pieces of paper into my notebooks, he tells me to meet him in the biology room. His messages get more and more urgent. I ignore them. Little worms of desire ooze from him as he walks past. Ever since I was autopsied on that table, I haven't felt like anything more than a corpse under his slimy gaze.

In fact, I'm dead.

In fact, I've disappeared under the shroud.

I don't know why my moving body keeps pretending when it would be better to give up.

It's like time's nervous tremor towards its own end. Days gone limp with warmth, days heavy with pollen, heavy with pollution, rains like drops of shadows drowning souls. Pale winters, as flat as the backs of our hands. Summers exploring bodies with burning hands. Cyclones and droughts one after another and speeding up. All that in a single year. The year I'm seventeen. Everything's happened to me: life and death.

I've lived many lives. And yet more I don't remember. Each of them has finished like this. Facing walls.

I see girls dancing and women walking along a carefully chosen path. I see pensive men and old guys happy with the sun on their white hairs. I see images on the television, shrill joy or morose suffering that bears no relation to what I am, to what I see. Why is nothing here in Troumaron like what happens on that screen?

I'm nothing. An accident along the way. A wasted thing. Singular, unified, eradicated.

The night devours me. Its gluttony is endless. Bit by bit, it gnaws, it nibbles. But it isn't done.

On the autopsy table, he remembers you. You or your shadow, either one. But he doesn't know anymore whether it's you or the other one, she who looked through the gap in the door that night.

He sets the books in order on the table. He doesn't like disorder. He lines up the edges. These are your own books. You left them for him. You didn't come back again. You don't want to smell the scents that stuck to them. Nor the images. Nor your face flattened between the pages.

On the biology table, he makes you last. He can do whatever he likes with your memory. A blue body, with soft innards. Purple lips, as if full of old blood. Arms so thin that they seem to have nearly disappeared. And at the end, a small damp hand that falls, lifeless, on the table's edge.

On the table that is his life, two girls have come back together. He cannot tell between them anymore. Equally beautiful and equally dead. He mixes the two of them up, their hands, their armpits, he watches them melt together, ever so slowly, into each other. Sometimes he's standing up, sometimes sitting, sometimes lying down. They slip from one place to another, switch places, and hang, like acrobats, in their pallor.

He is the happiest man in the world. On his knees, from his slowly aging body, from his days lost in not knowing when to live, from his futile attempts to communicate a knowledge he doesn't have, having become a man once more through the shiny depths of a body as flat as the table, a bone structure visible on the wood's dark face. The veins are its rivers. The shudders of this body taken by storm are the avenue down which he marches triumphantly, from the first day you offered him your downfall and your pitiless gaze. You offer what you have: a bit of nothing, a bit of everything.

Head banging against the wall under his ponderous rhythm. Did he see a warrior's gaze deep within your eyes? An avenging glare? He doesn't remember.

So much inertia. So much indifference. This "Monsieur" you bestow upon him after the act, and which nails everybody to the cross of their roles. That's all he is to you: "Monsieur." A teacher swallowed up by the impossibility of speaking.

He doesn't understand why other people fight for these little mummified beings who never break free. Others say: If one of them succeeds, that's a victory for them all. But when he comes into the classroom and sees the faces hardened under their masks of refusal, under their need for confrontation, under their defiance toward everything he has to offer, under their indifference to other prospects, he feels himself starting to die. He sets his books on the table as if slamming shut a coffin, knowing that what they contain emanates a sepulchral smell. He gets used to it right away. They see into him with such intensity, such cruelty that they instantaneously know how to hurt him. He snivels inside until the day a bit of sunlight on foamy hair shows him a hidden treasure in the back of the classroom, and his heart skips a beat.

In this moment, the color of his life changes: he's seen you. He discovers you, a small animal shirking behind your table, hanging on in order not to fall. You're surrounded by an inexplicable emptiness. When you leave, you leave alone, with an icy step. You're so thin he wants to carry you like a baby. You don't join in the heckling. You're isolated.

He only lives for you now, he loses himself in your night. Ever since he saw you, his life hasn't been the same. He's in limbo until he's with you again. But now you refuse him.

He's not made for this job. He's not made for anything. He spends

his life regretting his existence. Old before his time, with such scarce gifts.
Normalcy is long since past.
Day after day, everything breaks down.
Normalcy is in flight. How did it come to this?
He held a doll's body in his hands. He knew it wouldn't make him
happy. It was his revenge on life, against life, to break it in two.

EVE

He's a poor excuse for a father, he doesn't even know where to start with me. He ponders, he thinks, he wonders. Images float around and crash against his memories. A messed-up bed, a messed-up body, and too much woman for such a little girl.

A kid's love is passive. Then the clock starts ticking. The kid goes wild. What's a father supposed to do to bring his daughter to her senses? To keep her body from going crazy? To assert his power again? What power does he have over me, besides his violence?

Mother's drowning, kneading her flesh in despair all the while wishing she had an easier way to kill herself. She's just a small pile of shame at this point. Because of me she doesn't dare make herself seen anywhere. She knows me. She knows how far my defiance will go. How far I myself will go, not just to destroy myself, but to drag them along with me. A poor mother saddled with a girl so stubborn in her fury—isn't that what every mother dreads? Distrust burrows within her as well, the mother who couldn't take the reins and tame this wild blood, this surfeit of pride, this headstrong willfulness.

Children have wings of lead and keep thinking they can fly, until they're found, trash in a pile of trash.

The windows are filled with holes. The buildings go dark. The water doesn't run anymore. All friendly light is gone. The neighborhood is drowned in darkness. Nobody goes out. The increasingly nervous gangs gather weapons. A girl left dead and unavenged. A girl still rummaging through the ruins. Blood is called for. Only screams manage to tear through the emptiness.

Savita's parents are alone in their mourning. I think of them tonight. I want to tell them something about her, but my mere face would make them scream. They don't want to know me. They want to be alone with their dead body. But the final act has made their daughter unspeakable. Behind their horrified faces, the silent question etched in their eyes is this: what did she do to make this happen?

She is an active participant in her own murder. Even now she is still complicit. Even now she is her own murderer. This is how they feel.

The parents think, this was a normal girl, nothing special about her. They prize that as parents, a perfectly normal daughter. They don't know about the other side of her life, where she's written the most special and beautiful story of all. They can't possibly imagine the smile that swells her lips. They believed in her future and knew nothing about her present. Her present was me.

They look at the younger sister crying. Sobbing, shaking, their tears surging again. This time, it isn't for the older one but the younger one, as if they could already see, on the fresco of their terror, her shattered body.

I'm no longer prone to love. I'd like my heart to be flattened, as flat as my body, able to disappear when living becomes too hard.

I'm no longer prone to vertigo. I actually need to keep looking at the void again and again. From the roof where Clélio hides himself every so often, I look down into the depths. Deep down, something's waiting for me. My real shape. My arms starry wings. My legs spread wide. And my childlike face at rest, creamy with sadness and relief.

The only way to take flight is to take a step out.

To walk on a carpet of air, the consoling wind in my ears and the sun wending across the deep blue of the sky. The shriek weaving through my lips isn't a shriek of fear but of life.

A step out, a definitive decision. Space tamed. Just enough time to comprehend the briefness of eternity.

A step away from everything, from everybody, even myself.

Whatever's waiting deep down is just an unremarkable fluke. The little news item we don't think twice about, because it's just about small, wholly unreadable parts of ourselves. All the beginnings that have not ended are collected here, in a clenched fist.

I'm no longer prone to regret. That would mean wasting precious time when I could be living. But the only real question is: Am I prone to life?

CLÉLIO

It's dark. I'm stuck. This place is a hole. They're not hurting me, but I know I'm not getting out. My life stops here. I don't understand what happened. I know prisons well, but this is the first time I've ever felt like I'm fucked. They don't look at me like they did before. The policemen and wardens won't meet my eyes. In the papers there are already headlines: Savita's Presumed Murderer Taken into Custody. I can see the front page when the warden reads the paper. I see a picture of Savita, happy as always, smiling, half teasing, I'm telling you, like she's laughing at us all. And a picture of me: a repeat offender, of course, as if I could be anything else.

But I'm making plans in case I get out. I'll find a job, for real. I'm done acting stupid. Done acting like I want to punch everybody's face. Done acting like I have to be seen no matter what. I'm going to make myself as small as I can and stay out of trouble. I'm leaving the gang. I'm not chewing my fingernails anymore. I'm not shaving my head anymore. I'm scrubbing my tattoos with acid. I'm done carving Carlo into my skin.

Carlo was right to leave. That was what he had to do to escape. Break all ties with the past, otherwise it'll hold you back and never let you leave. Carlo, my brother, was right. He didn't come back to get me, but he left for me. To show me that it was possible. Even if he has a Renault, I forgive him. Even if he lies to Mam when he says that he has a house with ten rooms, I forgive him. He can't do it any other way. Leave, forget Troumaron, forget that he once lived here, that he once almost died here. Savita, too, she should have left. She didn't have time to. But we weren't the ones who killed her.

And my father, I have to understand why he's like that, too. The house we had before the hurricane, he and Mam bought it themselves. They paid for it all at last, and, even if it didn't look like much, even if it was as shaky as their heads, it was their own home. So when the hurricane destroyed it and they lost everything, it wasn't possible for them to begin again. My mother coped somehow. All mothers are like that. But he, he couldn't. Got to understand that.

Looks like I'm becoming a saint in prison. I'm starting to understand everyone. I'm not thinking about myself anymore. I'm thinking about Saad, that poor little dickhead in love with Eve. But no, he isn't a dickhead. If you're not in love at seventeen, when are you ever going to be able to fall in love? I think that's my problem right there. I've never loved. I haven't met anyone. Maybe I haven't bothered, maybe I've been too busy being angry.

But if I become a saint, maybe I might have to become a priest when I get out. And if I become a priest, I won't be able to fall in love again. So, it's better if I don't change too much. Besides, I just have to look at the warden's mug to know that I haven't changed all that much: I still want to murder him.

It's dark. I have to try to sleep. My thoughts are like those swarms of killer bees or cockroaches in a horror movie. As soon as I shut my eyes, they come out from every hole and climb all over me. They jump on me and begin nibbling at me everywhere. I shake them off, I scream, I throw my arms around enough to scare the other prisoners, but I can't get rid of them.

If I get out, I'll fuck the first woman I see. Well, if she's not too ugly. And not if she's my mother, what kind of person do you think I am?

EVE

The inspector finally agreed to take me to the morgue. I don't know how he did it, but he managed to get me in. He must have connections. That, and he feels sad for me. I don't care how he did it, I just care that I'll get to see Savita.

In the morgue, both the light and smell are greenish. I thought the movies would have prepared me for this. But movies have nothing to do with reality. It's totally different here. The filth in the corners. The ceiling blooming with mold. Chemical smells coming from the walls.

My whole body goes weak. The place is heavy with their presence. Everybody who came through here has left traces. On the walls, on the ground, on the ceiling, in the air. Like invisible lips sealed to their silence. Nobody ever leaves completely.

The inspector holds me by my arm and says, you don't have to.

No, I've never had to.

I shake my arm free. I don't want to turn back. After what she's gone through, I can go through everything. And then, in my head, I saw her a thousand times like this. I keep seeing her, in that envelope of death. And now I actually do see her.

Unmoving and pale. Her face glazed, rigid, solid. The bruises still on her neck from the murderer's fingers. I know her, yet she is wholly unrecognizable. Her youthfulness, I think. When death comes to someone so young, it makes her unrecognizable. And there's a bluish, almost purplish tint to her skin. I reel from the strangeness of it all.

But I do recognize her mouth. I hold on to that. That mouth

with its darkened edges is her mouth, Savita's mouth, I'm happy to see it again in all its perfection at last, yes, I haven't started to forget her features like I'd feared a second ago, I haven't betrayed her, I still have that memory of her mouth in me as something so precious that, for the rest of my life, all my senses will bring it back to me.

I explain to her that I was by the stream, and that was the reason I didn't hear anything. I tell her that for me, it's life that's distorting my features and making me unrecognizable.

My hand touches her cheek. I lean in, but the inspector holds me back. No, he says.

He takes me to a small café where the flies are more plentiful than the diners. I want for him to tell me something, for him to ask for something in exchange for the service he's rendered. He doesn't ask for anything. But he asks me questions. By the dirty window, I see the world going by. Yes, there's a world, over there, out there, that doesn't know Savita and where lives haven't stopped along with hers. I tell him everything, without really knowing why. How old I was when I began, where I went. I describe these places he knows so well. His questions take me further and further. My actions are getting crazier, I can tell. That's what he thinks: this girl is crazy.

He looks at me as if he can't believe me:

And you're still alive? he says.

What was the use of it all? he asks, again. His big hands on the table are trembling and fiddling with a paper napkin to the point that there aren't anything but shreds left. I wouldn't like to be a criminal he'd arrested. There isn't any skin that would resist those hands.

I finally answer his question:

To slip through the cracks. To...

To what?

To go on.

The next question had to be, go on to where, but he doesn't ask it. His eyes are tired and my thoughts are completely blank. I was thinking about buying myself a life. But I don't know which one.

He asks me if I have any health problems. I know what he's talking about, but I pretend not to understand. I show him the blue bruise on my cheek, which has turned yellow: these sorts of problems, yes, every day, I say.

He isn't looking at me anymore, I think he's trying to imagine what they did to me, what they made me do, what they'll make me do again, in the mirror behind the bar I see us and I know I look young, too young, a bit of string, a little burned thing, and I know he'd like to keep me from slipping further down, but he doesn't know anything at all.

Suddenly, he gets angry:

What if I shoved you in prison for a bit of time, you'd have to stop, that'd make you get better, wouldn't it?

I get up to leave. The conversation's over. There's nothing else to say.

It's hard to keep believing, he says quietly. But you have to defend yourself. I want you to stay alive.

He takes me back to Troumaron. In the car I don't say anything. But I remember something he said: Savita wasn't raped. I think he said that to reassure me. But then why was she killed? There was no anger there, no sexual violence. For the fun of it? Or to shut her up?

We pull up in front of the buildings. The sky is low. Here, there's always something watching. Some spirit that's vibrating, living, malignant.

He comes and opens the door of the jeep for me. I'm not used to that. Before I step down, he slips something into my bag.

Only use it to protect yourself, understand? he says very quietly.

I look down. I don't know why he did that. I didn't give him anything.

He holds me by the shoulders as I step down, and rubs them a bit.

He's talking in English. Be good, he says.

I shrug. It's too late to be good.

It's only once he's gone that I realize that we were right in the middle of all the buildings. Every window's facing us. Everybody saw me come back to Troumaron in a police car, everybody saw the inspector whispering in my ear. I colluded with the enemy. As usual, I'd done what I shouldn't have. I can almost hear through these windows what everybody must be thinking furiously: this time she went too far.

The ground starts to give way beneath my feet and caves in just as I walk into my apartment building.

But, after all, there was never any ground under my feet.

A light touch. Was there one? Maybe. Maybe not. The scene could have played out a thousand ways:

coming to open the jeep door, he picked you up like some straw, like a stalk, his big hands wrapping around your waist, he set you on the ground like something breakable

coming to open the door, he hid your half-naked body under his police vest, you had blue bruises on your arms

coming to open the door, he leaned in toward you and listened to the secrets unfurling like a pale mist from your mouth

coming to open the door, he laughed a little, knowingly, as if to say that we just have to behave ourselves, and you, too, laughed a little.

From window to window, fury flits around like a wild bird and bangs against the window panes to the point of breaking them.

The man is your fate and your death.

Coming to open the door, he put Troumaron's fate into your hands.

All around, the doors shut with the violence of a maimed laugh.

SAAD

That's the inspector we met together. She went to see him again. She came back with him. Eve, Eve, will you ever stop? Did you even manage to see Savita? What difference did it make, to have seen her body? She wasn't there, in the body, was she? What you saw was something else: a mask that could just as well have been your own.

I turn around in my cage. I spew my dark musings on the walls.

Maybe you wanted to make it up to her because she always waited for you after school and walked home with you? She thought she was protecting you, but you put her at far greater risk. She had nothing to do with your doings.

I mentally follow their path. I see them going home, both of them, afterward. After Eve was with the other guy. It's dark. Who follows them? Who waits for them and then follows Savita and not Eve? Why Savita? Why not Eve? Was it just chance? What was the difference between them? What did they have in common?

The clock's ticking. I can't sleep. I have to understand.

And then I realize I know. Like Eve, I know.

The gang's waiting for me. I miss our nighttime drives on motorbikes and mopeds. The night unfurls its fringes and we drink in the sharp scent of the neighborhood and our hot bodies are red-blooded shrieks of energy. It's a primal moment. A minute that explodes, that makes us all believe in living. For a minute, for an instant: living like a note drawn from a guitar, out of tune, but heard at a distance. Not disappearing. Not refusing to be.

But I don't go with them, because I know what they're talking about right now. There aren't that many possibilities. I saw how angry they got when she came back with this cop. How could she have been so stupid? Coming back here in a police car. She didn't even think. She only thinks about whatever's got her upset. Other people don't even cross her thoughts. I know her too well, this girl I dreamed up.

She wants her time, her actions, her decisions, her body to herself. She refuses to be worthless. But none of that belongs to her. And that's what we all are, anyway: worthless.

Somewhere in the abandoned factory, something's brewing. A red light bathes the buildings, sweeps the sky, streaks the façades. As always, like zombies in a horror movie, something that could be from an entrail, or a cave, or a drainage hole, or a basement window, comes out. These are the monsters we made, broken bottles in their hands, ready to devour, ready to disembowel. Life, in an instant, takes on this enemy's face.

But when the enemy gives way, we come back together, hungry, wild-eyed.

They think about Clélio in prison. They think about Savita dead. They think about Eve with the cop. The equation is too obvious. She has to submit.

My Eve, who believes herself born with steel in her heart, doesn't know it's the shine and warmth of gold living in her, that she will never stop melting and fleeing, and that this molten girl will soon be nothing more than a shapeless, faceless puddle.

In the abandoned factory, they get together to decide on a plan of action. Troumaron should be barricaded, one of them says. No, we have to attack whoever's threatening Troumaron, say some

ANANDA DEVI

others. Let's set fire to the police headquarters. Let's smash some
factory windows. Flip over some cars. Show them who they're
dealing with. They don't get to make Clélio a scapegoat. We'll
force them to release him, otherwise they'll kill him in prison, it's
easier than waiting for a trial. We've seen all this before. They'll do
the same thing to us. After that they'll tell us we're all the same,
we're all killers, all any of us deserve is a wall around the neighborhood, a wall all the way around with no openings. They'll turn
Troumaron into our prison, our ghetto.

The joints and booze help, everybody's ready to fight against
being imprisoned. In the glimmer of gas lights, unaware of the
danger, they begin making Molotov cocktails. Cigarettes in their
mouths, they soak rags in gas and stuff them in bottle necks. The
energy of violence floods them.

But first, they say, but first we have to find her. She's the one
who started it all.

Now all their fury is aimed at one thing.

I write on the walls of my room with permanent marker as
fast as I can, as if ill, as if insane, filled with an urge to tell everything before I'm forgotten. It's a broken-up, shaky story, rooted
in bitterness and rage, but it's the only one I know. The lives of
guys like me, so simple that they break apart before even coming
together, so indistinct that they fade away before having achieved
anything. Their hopes scatter every morning like the dust on their
feet. Their deaths don't aspire to brighten stars and only call to
mind the bare space of a grave. And so a wall is there the minute
they look at you.

Whoever comes into my room will contend with another

mystery. But, at least, I've said what I had to say. Eve, you have to flee. I have to help you flee.

EVE

It's like someone committed suicide with an exhaust pipe in this room. As soon as I locked myself inside, I smoked everything I could reach. But the pain is still here. And I'm still here.

Once again, my hair is practically torn out of my scalp. But this time, he used it to bang my head against the wall. I don't know where I hurt anymore. I don't know where I've been hit or what I've been hit against. Everywhere.

I crush a thousandth cigarette on the linoleum dotted with holes and undress. I almost have to peel the clothes off my skin. I look at myself in the mirror. I'm shocked at my appearance: even with all this pain, I hadn't realized how much damage had been done. I slump down on the bed, looking in the mirror, I don't know what I look like. Like nothing, nothing at all. Is there still anything to recognize?

My skin is so many colors: yellows, blues, purples, blacks, reds. If I didn't hurt so much, I'd have laughed. I'm covered in all Harlequin's colors. I didn't know that I could have so many different complexions. But when I try to smile, it hurts. A small crack gapes in the corner of my mouth. Then inside. And then, suddenly, a hundred cracks burst open. I'm cracking apart.

I take a pair of scissors out of a drawer.

This is how my mother finds me: curled up, locked in solitude, holding scissors in my right hand.

For once, she's calm. She kneels in front of me and tries to loosen my fingers around the scissors, but she's not able to do it. My hands are clenched and hers quiver too much.

Leave me, I tell her.

I'm not letting you do that, she says.

She thinks that I'm going to try to kill myself with these stupid scissors.

I'm not going to butcher myself, I tell her. I just want to cut off my hair.

I saw my hair in the mirror: bursting out of my head like fireworks. Like comic-book characters when a bomb's exploded in their face.

She sits on the bed next to me. She strokes my hair. Maybe she's thinking about how often people grabbed it. As if that was the strongest part of my body, the place where my energy could be grasped and absorbed.

My hair's the most visible part of my femininity. That's why they all start there, that's where they hurt me most.

I can almost hear her whispering: I've abandoned you.

I must be hearing wrong. But she says it again, more clearly: I've abandoned you. No mother should ever do that to her children. I've been cowardly, I've gone weak.

She takes pajamas out of the armoire and helps me put them on. Then she says, give me the scissors, I'll do it.

She takes them and begins cutting my hair. It's hard, it's difficult, the hair squeaks, the scissors grind. The clumps fall, strand by strand. The sound suits me, dries the tears that could have fallen. This contact seems strange, my mother's nearness, after so many years. I try to remember when we had been this close. But it's too far away. The feel of her hand on my scalp is pleasant. There's something special about motherly hands, I think. But it's too late for me.

I can't surrender to them. I don't want to be consoled.

When she finishes cutting the thickest clumps, she goes to find her husband's razor and shaves my head bald.

I look in the mirror. This time, I manage to smile. I really do have a funny head. I've metamorphosed. I think I look like what I wanted to be: a lioness. A starving lioness in a godforsaken zoo rather than a queen of the savannas, but it doesn't matter. I'll take it anyway.

My mother can't bring herself to look at me.

When she leaves, the lioness puts on pants with a grimace. She takes her bag and goes out without making a noise, as she knows how to do, so that nobody will notice.

Outside, even though I'm limping, nobody pays me any attention. I've become invisible, barely human, the incarnation of a will that, all by itself, manages to keep me upright and urge me forward.

He waits for you. He knows you will come. He knows it with the apathy of the next breath. Things have gone too far. He doesn't see the point of his actions anymore. He knows you will know sooner or later; the spark in your spirit, in your memory.

He is sitting in front of the television, bathed in its white light, fidgeting in silence. You have been to his place before, to get books. You know where he lives. You will open the door and you will breathe in the scent of rat poison. You will think that he might have opted for this outdated way of committing suicide, such a difficult, painful way, and that you will see his green body contorted in pain, his face twisted into a grimace at life. But don't worry: he will not offer you such an image of himself.

He will say to you, sit down. You will look at the armchair's flowery, worn fabric, and you will stay standing.

He will walk toward you and hold you in his arms. Your head will not reach above his chest. Despite himself, he will feel a stirring in his gut and want to pull you in closer while remembering you; already a memory, already past, already too late.

Most of all, he will think of that time, that night, when things skittered and time turned inside out. When his face was deep down within you, you began to bleed. He saw this outpouring still warm as the depths from where it came, this fluvial offering with such a strange texture, at once thick and liquid, with a coppery taste, reddening his lips. He pulled away. He saw the trickle flowing slowly, not like a wound, but like a stigmata that had simply opened. Wholly unexpectedly, this woman's blood, this flow from a buried volcano, seemed sacred to him.

When he got up, you looked at him. You put your fingers on his mouth. *His lips were red. Red from you, you thought. As he looked down at you, perhaps he looked like a vampire. Perhaps he looked like a member of a diabolical sect that drank blood. Perhaps he looked like a truly primitive being that drank its mother's milk and blood. But you only thought of a child with lips reddened by guava juice.*

Despite the confusion he was experiencing, he saw the smile that had come so quickly to your eyes. He told himself, this is the first time you've shown something, even if it's just a hint of a smile. The first time that something passes between the two of you. Something more than what usually goes from body to body.

All sorts of possibilities that he had never envisioned until now—a future, a sun that you cracked open in his life, a curtain of darkness he had thought permanent being raised—all appeared to him in his idiocy, out of nothing more than this reflection of a shadow of a smile.

And then, at that moment, there was a movement close to the door. He turned and saw the light in the slit of the half-shut door turning dark. (How had he failed to check the door?) He immediately saw himself as if from outside: his mouth reddened by the intimate blood of a woman. His reversal was immediate. Shame had overcome him all at once.

Shame in himself, in having come this far. Shame in being ridiculed, if the story spread. Shame in humiliation, if he was fired. Undone by a simple story. What little he had made out of his life was about to fall apart.

He waited until you left. He looked through the window and he saw the two of you walking away. He followed you both. Then he followed Savita. He killed her without hatred, almost without violence. At one point, he felt as if she was willing. But maybe she was simply too weak.

The weakness of a female body, its lack of fighting strength. At the very first blow, they give up. What remains is a passionless thing, maybe not even a thing. An annihilation. A disappearance. But she was already dead long before, this little girl who was your friend, long before he put her in a trash bin while thinking that this was what they did, those guys who lived in this neighborhood, if they had to kill. (Careless, irrevocable contempt.) She died at the moment she saw a red flower bloom on his mouth. She died when she saw his sad eyes and she knew that he was not killing her out of hatred.

No, not out of hatred. But indifference is far, far worse. He didn't even regret it.

And now he waits for you. He knows you will come. He only wants to hold you in his arms as a gift in his final hours. He will inhale the vanilla of your skin and touch the light T-shirt you are wearing and shudder while thinking about everything under it. He will know that these are his last sensations as a man before dying in his turn.

CLÉLIO

The public defender they assigned me is so young I thought it was a joke. I didn't say anything, but she could see it on my face that I didn't think there was any point getting a lawyer if they were going to pick a baby with a brand-new bib and a baby bottle, who wouldn't even get dirty while eating or defending her clients.

Sure, she's cute, with her little bangs over her eyes, I didn't want to get her mad. After all, she would definitely be the first one I saw when I got out. Or maybe, whispered a nasty little voice like my own except cleverer, she'll be the last one I see before being locked up for good. Would I actually be sentenced to death? I can't remember anymore if they still kill people here. I don't think there have been executions since I was born, but what do I know? Has the death penalty been abolished? Well, has the death penalty been abolished in Mauritius?

She smiles at me: reassuring, fake. She whispers something about a mandatory sentence of forty-six years, but they'll be lenient, especially if you're *juvenile*, she uses the English word as if to hide the tremor in her voice. Then she looks at me to see if I've understood. Yes, I've understood, chère mademoiselle. I'm not a kid anymore, I'm a *juvenile*, as in a juvenile delinquent.

Once the pleasantries are over, she starts explaining things, and I can see that she knows what she's talking about. She's serious, focused, attentive. Suddenly, I start listening to her more carefully. She frowns when I tell her that my only witnesses are birds and rats, but when I tell her that I was in the middle of carving Carlo's name in my ass that night, she doesn't raise an eyebrow but says, that just might help us…If we want to plead insanity, for example. But I'm not crazy, I tell her. She says in a soothing tone: No, I don't think you're crazy, but only a bit psychologically unstable. With good reason.

What do you mean, with good reason?

She doesn't answer right away. Her little face scrunches up, goes almost as gray as the prison's walls. This silence is like a secret she's sharing with me. I don't understand it, but it shocks me. I'm about to respond without thinking, despite my precarious situation.

I know where you come from, she says. I came from there, too.

I blink slowly. I can't imagine her as a little girl from Troumaron or anyplace like that. I look over her body for the markings that show us for the losers we are, the proof that her dreams have already started to go to shit, but I can't see it anywhere on her. I only see a good girl who's done something with her life. But then again, anything's possible. That doesn't mean I'm going to tell her my secrets, though. Maybe she made it all up to get me talking. Besides, if she wants to plead insanity, it's all over. I'm not an actor. I can't pretend to be crazy.

After she leaves, the lights go out. The air she'd made a bit more bearable solidifies around me. She can't do anything, I know. I don't believe in anything anymore. The papers have already begun my trial. The warden gleefully reads snippets of articles out loud while clicking his fake teeth. I'm described as "a dangerous thug who's already been behind bars several times." Reliable sources come out of the woodwork to say as much. One of the headlines is: "From Petty Theft Straight to Murder?" They interviewed my mother. She started by saying *Ki mo pu dir u*…When a mother begins with What can I tell you? then there's no hope. I can just see how the talk fell apart after that. Even when he was a kid, he was hard to control. I tried everything, I'm telling you. His father and me, we did everything we could to set him on the straight and narrow. But he was sucked into this gang of lowlifes. Once they had him, we couldn't do anything. *Piti-la inn sanze, mo dir u.* We don't recognize him anymore. And so on. She doesn't know how much she's hurting me, my poor Mam. She thinks that the *missié ziz* will have more compassion for me and it won't be so painful.

But at least, Mam, at the very least you could have told them that you didn't think I was guilty. You could have told them that.

There isn't a single voice speaking up for me. And I've been hearing voices since I've been in here. The voices in my head won't stop. But I'm not crazy, nor a Saint Bernadette. When there are too many walls around you, and walls beyond those walls, then the voices start talking to you to keep you from falling apart.

I just hope it won't last too long. I don't know how much longer I can hold out.

I hope they'll give me a second chance.

If anyone's listening out there, I'd really like a second chance. Even if I have to become a priest.

SAAD

They stream out, one after another, they follow each other with the sound of shrill music, unmelodious but still hypnotic. They buzz like bumblebees on the hunt. Hungry wasps, angry bees, furious insects who have just sighted a rare blossom not far off: a whole summer gathered into a single moving body that the horde senses from afar using some sense unavailable to men. The man-insects, bumblebee-machines, sketch large circles, dance their zigzag dances under the damp moon.

On their motorbikes, mopeds, and bikes, they set off in search of Eve.

I turn around in my room, armed with my black marker. I feel absolutely useless and powerless. I keep trying to describe my state of being while I think, which distances me from my thoughts. I do my best, as if the person writing was outside myself, using metaphors and similes, stylistic devices that just gussy up the truth. Why not just write, the gang's gotten on their bikes and left the city? Why not just say, I'm scared that they'll find Eve? Why not just say, I'm scared?

I write in order not to go crazy. I think that I've already said that, too. I want to cry. About this and about everything, about my need to live at all costs, me, the child of Troumaron, about my calls for help that nobody hears, about everything bearing down on us, about everything we're being accused of, about everything that's silencing us, about everything that's gagging us, to say to say to say to say, for that I'll kill them myself, I'll go on the hunt, I'll destroy every person who wants to hurt Eve, and I'll make myself a news item they talk about on the television and in the papers, and then, once I'm in prison, I'll write my story and I'll write poems and I'll send them to a publisher and they'll take notice, the distance between myself and my writing will command everyone's respect and they'll all say isn't that delightful, isn't that marvelous, this disadvantaged kid who's taken Rimbaud as his model, isn't that a brilliant media and literary stroke, I'll become a media sensation, and on top of that they'll feel like they're taking care of people's needs, they'll use me as a model for the other neighborhood kids who completely fuck up, but most of all, I'll be heard and read, which is what counts, no matter how they take it and what they make of it, even if they exploit me, if that's what they want, all I want, personally, is to get my head out of the water, to escape my fate, to simply be.

But to do that I have to kill.

But before that, I have to find her.

I have to summon up my courage to leave. The air is still streaked by their departures. If they see me, they'll force me to say where she's gone.

Opening the door of my room is hard. Here was a corner where I could breathe. Here was my den and my dawn. But outside, there's no continuity. Everything's stopped. Everything is waiting. The world is closed off. We can't escape the circles etched by our needs. These circles that tell the rest of the world, we're not like you, our world isn't like yours, today, they imprison us more thoroughly than the state's own prisons.

There should always be the possibility of an exit. So I can dream of an escape, even by tricking myself, even by hoping against hope.

In the neighborhood, everything's at a standstill.

The gang's spread out in Port Louis looking for her. They're armed with Molotov cocktails. They want to find her first. The only thing they'll listen to is the hammering in their heads and the bitterness in their mouths. The first strike will be the harshest in the city's silence. The others, after, will be easy. The noise and the screams will strike fear into people. Some will try to flee. Others will barricade themselves. And the wave will surge easily enough. They'll be attacked. They'll attack. The sparks will fly everywhere. And then the conflagration will begin.

They don't know this. They're blinded by their desire for the impossible. They don't understand just how fragile their world is. How this act of stupid, teenage rage, of throwing a rock at a store window can set off shock waves that will be all but impossible to stop. Kids breaking things, sure; but behind them, there are wolves waiting to come out and tear everything apart.

They choose to forget that here, they're all bound together. And that when people look at them, before seeing their faces, they see labels that are there for life.

I don't want to be one of those waking up the volcano. This island was born from a volcano. One eruption is enough. I have to start running to find her before they do. Besides, I know where she is.

EVE

I limp, I hobble. Every breath is a door forced open. Each one lasts an eternity. Every breath awakens the numbest parts of my body. But this way, at least, I am sure I am conscious.

This will take as long as it has to. My time isn't like others'. The two things guiding me are freedom and the end.

All these broken breaths catch in my throat. There they begin to tighten. I think I can understand what Savita endured. Thinking of her hurts even more, now that I know that it really was because of me.

This man's hypocrisy makes me laugh, or scares me, I'm not sure. Oh, his tremors, his little jumps, his fears. A little, lizardly, spineless thing. He wanted me so much that he was able to overcome his shame. His courage was enough to bring him to the biology room and make his shadow on the walls into a naked monster; but being seen by someone else—oh, no, no. Another eye witnessing his degeneration, no. He could lay me flat on a table and shove me into the wood splinters, he could take me in every way, he could pretend to love me when we were alone in the prison of his fantasies. Until someone else sees us, and he denies everything. I can already hear him saying it, it was she who seduced me. She begged me. She threw herself on me. I ended up raping him, oh sure I did.

I think of the gun the inspector gave me, hitting my armpit every so often. He gave me a way to turn everything around. To wipe the slate clean. I've waited too long. There's a whole world beyond rules and regulations. Savita's body told me: burn your bridges and run. The inspector told me: this isn't to bury you, it's to clear a path for you. He knows which way I've been going, and where my next encounter by stone walls might take me.

I'll leave my mark right between his eyebrows. Then I'll leave. Violence as my escape. There's no other way out. In my bag, under my arm, the gun bobs around. My bargaining chip with fate. I don't need to take everything with me. I was stupid, as we all are at seventeen. Now, I know. There's a place where the birds' cries are short and piercing, and where summer burns so vividly that you'll forget even the memory of maggots in your guts.

Death is in your hands, says the gun in my bag.

So is life, says Savita.

What will you choose?

I summon up all the memories I can before looking into these eyes grown old before their time, this man driven by shame and impotence to murder. He is far more disconsolate than I ever will be.

CLÉLIO

A softness slips into her eyes, in the shadow of her bangs. For me?

Her name is Lauren.

Her name is Lauren.

I don't think I'll be sentenced to death.

I can take apart the bricks that buried me here. One by one, I can detach them from their mortar beds, even if I destroy my nails and my youth. As I keep staring at the walls, they become a dirty smudge, then a hole, then nothing. Open to everything. Collapse into nothingness.

Cry or laugh? The choices are limited.

But the most important thing is to be convinced: I didn't kill. The world can go to pieces. I didn't kill.

In the middle of the night, I make my way out of this sludge that passes for sleep here and I see through the bars that Carlo is looking at me. I jump to my feet. Carlo! You're back! He nods but he doesn't say anything so he doesn't upset me with his fake French accent. I look right at him and stick my hands through the bars. He holds my hands, but his are so cold that I shiver. Are you cold, Carlo? I ask him. He nods again. It's the prison air, I tell him. It'll chill you to death. Don't stay there. I'll come meet you outside. I take off my shirt and give it to him. When he puts it on, I see that he's naked and very thin. What's wrong, Carlo? And then I see he's also in a prison cell. I don't understand anything.

And then I'm outside. In a place that looks like Le Souffleur. I'm standing on the edge of a rocky cliff. The water spurts up and the waves crash against the sides of the cliff, wearing away at it, nipping at it. It seems like earlier the wind was whistling like a horn as it passed through the tunnels the water had carved in the rock. It sighed, it groaned, it could be heard in the nearby villages like dead people's voices. Until these waves widened these holes more and more and took away these voices of the wind and of the dead. So I'm the one screaming, sighing, groaning, and awakening this place from its silence.

In prison, only my voice can be heard now.

Then the sludge of sleep overcomes me again.

At night, they say that the oceans sleep. But maybe they're already dead.

SAAD

I am Saad, and I am my name. I enter sadness's downpour. I am the only person who can walk under a cloud of his own name.

It's raining. I'm cold from all this rain. I want to go with her, to go down her path, to go into her suicide; a pact, between two dying beings, two beasts exhausted before even starting to live.

But I don't want to stop here, either. I still have a life to live. I'm not afraid of stumbling. I'm afraid of the fall. What will happen to these boys and girls like me, like her, when the blade falls on their night, on their laughter. Haven't we all come this far, to this moment?

It's all so brief. A few pathetic years, barely enough time to open new eyes to our life, and already we're staring at death. Our alternatives: either defeat or violent conquest. But this conquest isn't really one. It's the resistance of the hopeless. That's what I wanted to tell them, they who are ranging right now across the city with their angelic yet malevolent faces, caught up in their fake rhythm, their machines' sputtering portending failure. I don't know what ties us to these murderous cadences.

Maybe the gray sunlight of our birth?

It's raining. It's raining in my head. It's raining everywhere in my secrets. You could say I'm crying, but that isn't true.

I don't want to die.

I want to talk about these places that exist outside time, that murder us. I mean these places that stubbornly repress all that we are.

I walk through a succession of armored and padlocked doors.

The farther I walk, the more I feel as if I am the one they are locking out. Nobody will let me back in again. I have abandoned every permitted space, all the normal places. Eve's the one who's dragged me along her inward path, into her hurricane of wrath.

I bump into sleeping bodies in the doorways. On the steps slick with rain, their features stripped bare, they sleep. Drunkards, fallen under the weight of alcohol in their bellies. A very old woman, possibly dead, a pile of rags under her head as a pillow. A dog and a man together, breathing in rhythm.

They all have the same face, as blank as their rips and tears. It feels like I could enter them and live in the heart of their sadness. I could be each of the furrowed wrinkles on the old woman's face. I could be the sick dog's flank, entering through his sides and trying to keep life flowing within his body. I could be the man's hand, moving—closed, open, closed, open—so he wouldn't freeze completely. I could be the hem of his frayed shirt soaking beside him in a puddle of urine. I could be the wind's voice sighing without any violence and the island sleeping without trying to understand.

If I can be all that, I can also be her, Eve. I know where she is, what she's doing. I've always known.

And I'm this wan, wretched man who's destroyed the city's peace, whose cowardice and urges have led to this explosion.

And I'm the fathers and mothers asphyxiated by the airless void of failure.

And I'm the furious, thirsty boys who think they'll free themselves by sowing discord.

And I am, like him, the one who talks to me in my dreams, a thief of fire.

But now, I am me: become again simple and double and multiple all at once. I am Saad. Nothing else matters.

You look at him and you are astonished by the transformation he has undergone. He is crushed by remorse. Like a worm, he tries to hide in the corners. In the open door, in his resigned gestures when you enter, his hand raised and then quickly lowered, you see that he's been expecting you. In front of him is a half-empty bottle of rum, its vapors filling the room and masking other, more permanent smells. Around him, there are sheets of paper, some of them torn, others not. There are pictures of someone who vaguely looks like him, made unrecognizable by hope. This person is someone whose light has flared.

You feel, just before you kill him, a brief twinge of pity. Then you steel yourself: he never felt the least pity himself. Cowardly, humiliated, selfish: all the more reason for him to disappear.

He attempts to get up, but he doesn't have the strength. In his uneven breath, you can see he's afraid. He says:

Don't hurt me.

These words strike an icy chill in your thoughts. Every time you met a man, in your soul, in your flesh, there were these words: don't hurt me. You never said them out loud. But you could never have known beforehand the extent of the damage. And you were hurt, they didn't hesitate, didn't flinch, sometimes smiled, sometimes seemed not to care. It was just, you thought, part of the bargain.

But today, it's the man who says them, just because you have a gun in your hand. You accept this reversal of roles. You welcome the contempt that fills your gut.

You tell him: get down on your knees.

That, too, they said to you every time. Get down on your knees.

Open your mouth. Take it.

He is so worn out that he seems about to disappear. He doesn't understand. You repeat:

Get down on your knees.

He does it. You walk up to him, you lift up his chin and you look him in the eyes, so as not to forget this face, this moment. Then you set the mouth of the barrel on his forehead, between his eyebrows.

The gun is heavy, but it's not very big and fits comfortably in your hand. You wonder if the safety is switched off, if you know how to shoot. The waxy skin you're looking down at doesn't look human at all. It looks more dead than Savita's skin at the morgue.

You think about her again, as you saw her last. It's because of him that she had this purplish tinge, this rigidity, this absolute stillness. It's because of him that she contradicts everything she ever was: a girl who was laughing, thoughtful, warm, and alive—above all, alive. He was her final moment. It was this face—pasty, defeated, unaware of the very meaning of the word love—that she saw at the moment she died.

You will not forgive him.

EVE

I left his place, astonished that nobody heard the noise. I hadn't expected it, this noise. I thought I would go deaf. But my hand hadn't trembled.

He looked like all the others behind his closed eyes.

I walk out into the rain that has begun to fall. It is slow and warm. It dampens my bare scalp, presses my clothes to my skin. It is so heavy that puddles form around my feet, grow, and swallow them up.

I feel like I've walked away from the house, but I see I haven't moved. I stay there, standing, not knowing what I should do.

How does the rest of the story go? Saad, that's your job, to tell it. I myself don't know. Will mine finish here, at seventeen? Is life really that short?

SAAD

It's done: I called the police to warn them about a possible riot. I hope they'll come in time.

I came running to the teacher's house. Eve is standing in front of the house. She's turned her back on it. She's completely soaked by rain. Even without her hair, I recognize her right away. Eve, it's Eve. She has a gun in her hand.

She's gripped by starlight. Her face looks like it's come undone. Odd colors, colors of blows and bruises cloud her features. Her eyes are so deep and their echoes so metallic that I have trouble meeting her gaze. They go beyond this house, beyond Port Louis, beyond the present. Her eyes see into tomorrow, and tomorrow doesn't exist.

The rain brings the odors of the sea. It falls all around her with a gentle rumble. The rain almost seems as if it could soften her and melt her, until there was nothing left of her.

I stop in front of her and I take the gun from her hand. She doesn't stop me. She says:

He left a letter, about Savita.

I say, good, they'll have to release Clélio, and besides, that gives me an excuse.

An excuse?

When I go to turn myself in to the police.

She shakes her head and explains, calmly: No, I'm the one who killed him, not you.

Eve, I say, let me do it. I know what I have to do.

She looks at me with what little of her wrath remains:

I have to go all the way, it has nothing to do with you.

I drag her to a low wall that will protect us a bit from the rain. I force her to sit down next to me. She is so exhausted and shaky that she lets me do it, even if moving reawakens all her pain and makes her wince.

I don't want you to take the blame for me, she says. I forbid you from doing it.

I don't need you at all.

I don't need you at all.

Six words: one for each hand, one for each foot, one for the head, and one for the heart. I drip red.

For the first time, she wraps her arms around me. Her mouth is desolate, but inflexible. Despite my dismay, I think of the inch separating us.

Otherwise it won't have been of any use, she says.

I don't know what use it was. I can feel her halting breath, her uneven heartbeat.

I look at the damage wreaked upon her body. She is sculpted like volcanic rock. I don't understand violence at all: it is there, everywhere. A poison floating in the air.

But I am sure of one thing: for her, with her, for one season or many, I am ready to go into hell. Nothing else matters. I stroke the nape of her neck, her bare head. Even under the low wall, the water is drowning us.

But the rain tastes sweet on her lips.

TRANSLATOR'S AFTERWORD

To call Mauritius part of Africa feels simplistic: the tiny island is actually on the other side of Madagascar from the rest of the continent, deep within the Indian Ocean. It has been colonized successively by Dutch, French, and British explorers, and, despite becoming an independent democracy in 1968, traces of its colonial history can be seen everywhere, from the various historical buildings around the capital city of Port Louis to the numerous ethnicities—Western European, Eastern African, Indian, and Chinese—that became part of the island's population as settlers, slaves, indentured servants, and, finally, immigrants. This history is also evident in Mauritius's languages: when the British took over the island, they allowed the inhabitants to keep using French, and to this day most Mauritians are fluent speakers of English, French, and Mauritian Creole.

This mélange of languages, cultures, and histories parallels Ananda Devi's own background. She was born in Trois Boutiques on the southeastern end of the island, and grew up in a family of Indian heritage. By the age of fifteen, she was already winning prizes for her short stories, and she continued to write prolifically even as she moved to England for a PhD in Anthropology and to Congo-Brazzaville for work before finally settling in France by the Swiss border. These various influences and interests have shaped her literary career, as she has trained her novelistic gaze on disenfranchised populations and the ways in which femininity is shaped and established. Her gorgeously hewn sentences rarely shy away from depicting violence or suffering; her novels, rather, embrace the entirety of human experience, from abject suffering to unalloyed joy.

Devi's prose reveals the complexity of the country she still returns to every year, and I quickly came to realize that *Eve Out of Her Ruins* would present intriguing challenges as I translated it. Devi writes in French purely by choice, and the sentences her Mauritian narrators speak or write bear tinges of English and Mauritian Creole. English syntax occasionally creeps in, which I mirrored with snippets of French syntax. Foreign words and phrases stand out vividly on the page, and just as I kept Mauritian Creole phrases intact, so I kept occasional French words like *cité* (ghetto) unchanged from the original.

There are a few multilingual puns. The neighborhood, for example, is named Troumaron, and French speakers might recognize the Creole name as meaning *trou marron*, or "brown hole." The implication in Mauritian Creole, of course, is much dirtier. Another pun is visible as one of the narrators says his name: "Je suis Sadiq. Tout le monde m'appelle Sad." Someone reading the French text likely would catch the reference to the English emotion, just as a knowledgeable English reader might notice the parallel pun in a man saying "I am Tristan. Everybody calls me Triste." To maintain a similar subtlety, I retransliterated the name from the Arabic word for "truth" and "friend": "I am Saadiq. Everybody calls me Saad."

Eve Out of Her Ruins is a harrowing story, but even its most intense moments of grief are tempered by the beauty of Devi's prose. As I've translated it, it's been my pleasure to meet so many readers that this book has touched in French. Annabel Kim was the first to press the novel upon me. Professor Thomas C. Spear, who maintains the Île en île website dedicated to Francophone writers, has been an invaluable ally and advocate. The generous editors at *The Offing*—Amanda DeMarco, Charles Lee, and Darcy Cosper—published the first pages of this book and helped it to find a home in print. Justin Dickinson spent a long afternoon poring over sentences with me, and provided me with insights that lingered over the rest of my work. Similarly, Cécile Menon and Angeline Rothermundt gave this translation one of the most thorough, thoughtful edits I could have asked for. And it is thanks to the efforts and passion of Cécile Menon, Charles Boyle, and Will Evans that Ananda Devi's stunning novel is being brought, at long last, to a new cadre of readers in English.

And I owe a debt of gratitude to Ananda Devi herself for answering so many questions, teasing out new interpretations, imbuing this translation with her own singular voice, and—most of all—writing such an extraordinary book.

Jeffrey Zuckerman

ANANDA DEVI was born in 1957 in Trois-Boutiques, Mauritius, an island notable for its confluence of diverse ethnic, cultural, and linguistic identities. She studied ethnology and anthropology, and completed a doctoral thesis at SOAS in London. After several years in the Congo, she moved to Switzerland in 1989. She has published eleven novels as well as short stories and poetry over her entire career. *Eve Out of Her Ruins*, originally published by the prestigious Gallimard publishing house in France in 2006, was an enormous critical and popular success, winning the Prix des cinq continents de la francophonie for the best novel of the year written in French, previously won by such writers as Alain Mabanckou and Mathias Enard. She was made a Chevalier des Arts et des Lettres by the French Government in 2010. Her first novel in English, *Indian Tango*, was published by Host Publications in 2011, and she has been a part of numerous literary festivals in the US, Europe, and India, and her works have been translated into numerous languages.

JEFFREY ZUCKERMAN is Digital Editor at Music & Literature magazine and a translator from French. He has served on the 2016 jury for the PEN Translation Prize, and his translation of Antoine Volodine's *Radiant Terminus* is forthcoming from Open Letter in 2017. His writing and translations have appeared in Best European Fiction, the *Los Angeles Review of Books*, the *Paris Review Daily*, the *New Republic*, and *VICE*.

JEAN-MARIE GUSTAVE LE CLÉZIO was born in April 13, 1940 in Nice, France, but both parents had strong family connections with the former French colony of Mauritius. He is president and long-standing member of the prize jury for the Prix des cinq continents de la francophonie (awarded to Ananda Devi's *Eve Out of Her Ruins* in 2006), and he was awarded the Nobel Prize for Literature in 2008.

Thank you all
for your support.
We do this for you,
and could not do
it without you.

DEEP
VELLUM

DEAR READERS,

Deep Vellum Publishing is a 501c3 nonprofit literary arts organization founded in 2013 with the threefold mission to publish international literature in English translation; to foster the art and craft of translation; and to build a more vibrant book culture in Dallas and beyond. We seek out literary works of lasting cultural value that both build bridges with foreign cultures and expand our understanding of what literature is and what meaningful impact literature can have in our lives.

Operating as a nonprofit means that we rely on the generosity of tax-deductible donations from individual donors, cultural organizations, government institutions, and foundations to provide a of our operational budget in addition to book sales. Deep Vellum offers multiple donor levels, including the LIGA DE ORO and the LIGA DEL SIGLO. The generosity of donors at every level allows us to pursue an ambitious growth strategy to connect readers with the best works of literature and increase our understanding of the world. Donors at various levels receive customized benefits for their donations, including books and Deep Vellum merchandise, invitations to special events, and named recognition in each book and on our website.

We also rely on subscriptions from readers like you to provide an invaluable ongoing investment in Deep Vellum that demonstrates a commitment to our editorial vision and mission. Subscribers are the bedrock of our support as we grow the readership for these amazing works of literature from every corner of the world. The more subscribers we have, the more we can demonstrate to potential donors and bookstores alike the diverse support we receive and how we use it to grow our mission in ever-new, ever-innovative ways.

From our offices and event space in the historic cultural district of Deep Ellum in central Dallas, we organize and host literary programming such as author readings, translator workshops, creative writing classes, spoken word performances, and interdisciplinary arts events for writers, translators, and artists from across the world. Our goal is to enrich and connect the world through the power of the written and spoken word, and we have been recognized for our efforts by being named one of the "Five Small Presses Changing the Face of the Industry" by Flavorwire and honored as Dallas's Best Publisher by D Magazine.

If you would like to get involved with Deep Vellum as a donor, subscriber, or volunteer, please contact us at deepvellum.org. We would love to hear from you.

Thank you all. Enjoy reading.

Will Evans
Founder & Publisher
Deep Vellum Publishing

LIGA DE ORO ($5,000+)

Anonymous (2)

LIGA DEL SIGLO ($1,000+)

Allred Capital Management
Ben & Sharon Fountain
Judy Pollock
Life in Deep Ellum
Loretta Siciliano
Lori Feathers
Mary Ann Thompson-Frenk
  & Joshua Frenk
Matthew Rittmayer
Meriwether Evans
Pixel and Texel
Nick Storch
Social Venture Partners Dallas
Stephen Bullock

DONORS

Adam Rekerdres
Alan Shockley
Amrit Dhir
Anonymous
Andrew Yorke
Anthony Messenger
Bob Appel
Bob & Katherine Penn
Brandon Childress
Brandon Kennedy
Caroline Casey
Charles Dee Mitchell
Charley Mitcherson
Cheryl Thompson
Christie Tull
Daniel J. Hale

Ed Nawotka
Rev. Elizabeth
  & Neil Moseley
Ester & Matt Harrison
Grace Kenney
Greg McConeghy
Jeff Waxman
JJ Italiano
Justin Childress
Kay Cattarulla
Kelly Falconer
Linda Nell Evans
Lissa Dunlay
Marian Schwartz
  & Reid Minot
Mark Haber

Mary Cline
Maynard Thomson
Michael Reklis
Mike Kaminsky
Mokhtar Ramadan
Nikki & Dennis Gibson
Olga Kislova
Patrick Kukucka
Richard Meyer
Steve Bullock
Suejean Kim
Susan Carp
Susan Ernst
Theater Jones
Tim Perttula
Tony Thomson

SUBSCRIBERS

Aldo Sanchez

Amber Appel

Anonymous

Barbara Graettinger

Ben Fountain

Ben Nichols

Bill Fisher

Bob Appel

Brandye Brown

Cheryl Thompson

Chris Sweet

Courtney Marie

David Weinberger

Ed Tallent

Frank Merlino

Greg McConeghy

Ines ter Horst

James Tierney

Jeanne Milazzo

Jennifer Marquart

Jeremy Hughes

Jill Kelly

Joe Milazzo

Joel Garza

John Winkelman

Julia Rigsby

Julie Janicke

Justin Childress

Kenneth McClain

Kimberly Alexander

Lara Smith

Lissa Dunlay

Lytton Smith

Marcia Lynx Qualey

Margaret Terwey

Martha Gifford

Michael Elliott

Michael Holtmann

Neal Chuang

Nhan Ho

Nick Oxford

Owen Rowe

Patrick Brown

Peter McCambridge

Rainer Schulte

Robert Keefe

Scot Roberts

Shelby Vincent

Steven Norton

Susan Ernst

Tim Kindseth

Todd Mostrog

Tom Bowden

COMING FALL/WINTER 2016–2017 FROM DEEP VELLUM

CARMEN BOULLOSA · *Heavens on Earth*
translated by Shelby Vincent · MEXICO

ANANDA DEVI · *Eve Out of Her Ruins*
translated by Jeffrey Zuckerman · MAURITIUS

JÓN GNARR · *The Outlaw*
translated by Lytton Smith· ICELAND

CLAUDIA SALAZAR JIMÉNEZ · *Blood of the Dawn*
translated by Elizabeth Bryer · PERÚ

JOSEFINE KLOUGART · *On Darkness*
translated by Martin Aitken · DENMARK

SERGIO PITOL · *The Magician of Vienna*
translated by George Henson · MEXICO

EDUARDO RABASA · *A Zero-Sum Game*
translated by Christina MacSweeney · MEXICO

BAE SUAH · *Recitation*
translated by Deborah Smith · SOUTH KOREA

DEEP
VELLUM